the Messenger

Books by T. Davis Bunn

The Quilt
The Gift
The Messenger

The Maestro
The Presence
Promises to Keep
Riders of the Pale Horse

The Priceless Collection
Secret Treasures of Eastern Europe

1. *Florian's Gate*
2. *The Amber Room*
3. *Winter Palace*

Rendezvous With Destiny

1. *Rhineland Inheritance*
2. *Gibraltar Passage*
3. *Sahara Crosswind*
4. *Berlin Encounter*
5. *Istanbul Express*

the Messenger

T. DAVIS BUNN

BETHANY HOUSE PUBLISHERS
MINNEAPOLIS, MINNESOTA 55438

Bun

Cover illustrations by Andrea Jorgenson.
Inside illustrations by Lorraine Major.

Copyright © 1995
T. Davis Bunn

Published by Bethany House Publishers
A Ministry of Bethany Fellowship, Inc.
11300 Hampshire Avenue South
Minneapolis, Minnesota 55438

Printed in the United States of America.

Library of Congress Cataloging-in-Publication Data

Bunn, T. Davis, 1952–
    The messenger / T. Davis Bunn.
        p.   cm.

    1. Angels—Fiction. I. Title.
PS3552.U4718M47   1995
813'.54—dc20   95–482
ISBN 1–55661–669–4   CIP

To Bill and Cathy Delay

Disciples of Prayer,
Teachers of Rightful Living,
Friends.

"And now at last this Good News has been plainly announced to all of us. It was preached to us in the power of the same heaven-sent Holy Spirit who spoke to them; and it is all so strange and wonderful that even the angels in heaven would give a great deal to know more . . ."

1 PETER 1:12, TLB

*M*y goodness, dear, do come sit down. You're making me nervous just watching you."

"Oh yes, sorry, of course." The young woman in the crisp starched uniform settled down with the fluttering motions of a nervous robin. "I'm just so excited."

The older woman smiled. "First time, is it?"

"Yes, yes, very first." She cast quick glances about the transition hall, seeing everything and nothing. "I've been dreaming about this chance, but I never thought it would come so soon. I'm only halfway through my training."

"Well, it certainly is nice to see someone so eager. There's altogether too much grimness in the departure lounges these days, if you ask me."

"Why is that?"

"Never you mind," the older woman

7

replied gently. "Do you have your assignment?"

"Oh yes, and my sachet of blessings."

"I beg your pardon?"

"Right here around my neck." She released her top button and pulled on the thin gold chain. "See?"

"How remarkable," the old woman murmured.

"And my pass is in my pocket."

"Your—what did you say?"

She dug deep into her uniform, came up with a slender card that shimmered like a sheet of burnished silver. Her face dominated by solemn eyes, she said, "They told me that I can't be too careful with this."

The older woman leaned her head down, her eyes closed in quiet repose. There was a sense of gathering stillness before the dark face rose once more. She said quietly, as to herself, "What a vital message for both of them."

"Excuse me," the young woman said, her tone touched by reverence. "Were you praying?"

The older woman's smile shone brilliant against the cast of her dark skin. "You had difficulty with the lessons on prayer, did you?"

She gave a shy nod. "I tried to learn everything, truly I did."

"But it seems confusing, since the Father has always been with us. I do understand," the older woman finished for her. "And yet here in this way station the first glimmer of how important this lesson truly is begins to show forth." She gave the young woman's hand a soft pat. "Just be sure you remember the lessons they gave you. Otherwise our home here can seem awfully distant at times."

The pretty forehead creased in worry. "But how is that possible, since He is everywhere and always?"

"Never you mind." The older woman said again with a reassuring smile and changed the subject. "Where are you going?"

"Philadelphia." She said the name slowly, as if the sounds were alien to her mouth. "That's a city."

"Indeed it is. And where will you be serving?"

"Someplace called a hospital," she said, and named the date.

"Oh yes. A good starting point," the old woman assured her. "I am traveling to a hospital as well, and at the same period."

Eyes widened even further. "You are? Oh, that's wonderful. Perhaps we could meet and you could show me what—"

"I would love to, my dear," the older woman said gently. "But unfortunately there is more than one hospital."

"Oh," the young lady said, crestfallen. "I didn't know that."

"I am sure you will do just fine." The old woman patted her hand. "What service are you called to perform?"

"People have been praying for aid to a woman in need."

"Oh yes. That is a happy occasion, being sent to answer a prayer. Well, stand up and turn around, let me look you over. Can't be too careful. Why, I once almost traveled to twentieth-century Egypt dressed in a Parisian frock from the gay nineties. Imagine what a fuss that would have caused."

The young lady looked helplessly confused. "I don't think I understand anything you just said. And I've already forgotten what a century is."

"Oh, dear, listen to me prattle on, and here it is your first journey. Don't worry, dear. Some things can only be learned through experience."

"Oh, please tell me. I'm so anxious to get it right, but it's all so strange, you know."

"My, how refreshing you are to be with," the old woman exclaimed. "Sit back down, dear. You look just fine." When the young woman was settled, her new acquaintance went on, "I know it is strange, my dear. But you see, where we are going there is a thing called time."

"Yes, they told us about that. I'm afraid I didn't understand it very well."

"No one does, dear. Not until they've experienced for themselves, and even then it remains quite confusing. In any case, a century is a measurement of time."

The young lady brightened. "I learned about measures. Feet, inches, miles. A century is how many miles?"

The old woman smiled fondly. "You do my heart good, child. I had almost forgotten what my own first trip down was like."

"What do you mean, down?"

"You will find that out soon enough." The old woman's smile took on a forced quality. "Home can appear quite distant, I'm afraid. But take it in stages, that's the proper way."

"What will you be doing?"

"Oh, I've quite a task ahead of me. I'm going to a hospital in Washington—that's a city south of Philadelphia. It is called the Saint Mark Hospice for the Dying, a place for the critically ill. There is a splendid young girl who is to be called home in a rather difficult way. She is what they call an orphan and will be needing someone to remind her what love is. I'm to be there until she departs, perhaps as long as a week."

"A week?"

"Dear me, there I go again. A week is another measurement of time."

"Oh, I remember now. Three hundred and sixty-five weeks make a century, except in leap month."

The woman reached over and squezzed the young lady's hand. "You'll do just fine, dear. Now you must promise to come look me up when we're back. My name for the moment is Miss Simpkins."

"I am Ariel," the young lady replied, then jumped when the gong sounded. "Oh, that's the signal."

"Go in peace, dear," Miss Simpkins said, rising to her feet. "And no matter what happens or what you see, remember whom you serve. Draw near to His presence, and draw His presence near to you, in prayer."

*M*anny was the best in the business, ask anybody. Slick as an eel, fast as a speeding bullet. Nights on the prowl, he wore a black cape emblazoned with his own form of the superhero's symbol, a fist holding a lightning bolt. Whenever anybody mentioned that the emblem was used by some military unit, Manny always got hot, claimed they stole it from him.

Manny liked to copy tricks he saw on television, practice them until they were smooth, then play at casual when the nightspot crowds egged him on between music sets. It was his trademark, his way of making a name in the night world he relished. That and the rumors that swirled and followed him about. His latest trick was to juggle a bowling ball, a sharpened kitchen knife, and an apple. As he juggled, he ate the apple. That really wowed them. Yeah, Manny had great hands. Ask anybody.

He could probably have made pretty good

money as a performer. But that wasn't
Manny's gig. He lived for the forbidden high,
the ecstasy of danger, the thrill of tightrope
tricks nobody but Manny ever saw.

Manny was a pickpocket. A master. A pro.

That day, however, he really wasn't intent
on working. He'd had some rich pickings the
past few days. He was loitering outside the
diner where he always had breakfast on slow
days, across the street from the hospital's emer-
gency room entrance. He was trading jibes with
the paramedics, adrenaline junkies to a man.
Then the pigeon appeared.

That was how he always thought of them.
Pigeons. Birds too stupid to get out of the way,
cluttering up the streets, clutching at the
crumbs of life. And this one was a trip.
Dressed in a candy striper's uniform so
starched she crackled with each step. Staring
wide-eyed up at the hospital like she'd never
seen one before in her life. Jumping three feet
off the sidewalk when an ambulance did a
four-wheel skid around the corner. Gasping
when one of the grifters shuffled over and
tried to sell her a pair of cheapo sunglasses.
Spinning about and smiling shyly at the paramedics when they called out an invitation for

her to come over, have a coffee, listen to the story of their lives.

Manny pushed himself off the wall. He popped his head so that his shades fell forward and down over his eyes, then sauntered over. Broad daylight, in front of maybe a dozen guys, cops popping in and out of the ER entrance all the time. Definitely one for the books.

She gasped again when he slid up on silent feet, took hold of her elbow, said, "You don't watch it, they're gonna be working *on* you instead of with you. Know what I mean?"

"I . . .oh yes, this is the hospital?" She gave him a smile too sweet for somebody who could ever know the law of the streets. "I must go there."

"You foreign, right? Yeah, shoulda known, that hair and the accent. Your first day in the fast lane?"

"I'm sorry, I don't think I—"

"Hey, no sweat. C'mon, lemme show you the ropes." The grip on her elbow shifted to his other hand, so that he was walking with half his body a scarce millimeter off of hers, urging her forward, protecting his own slick motions from the view of those standing behind making jealous catcalls as Manny made his move. Not understanding that somebody like Manny had no use for the pigeons of this earth, other than to take and run.

Pocket. It all had to be in her pocket. She wasn't even carrying a purse.

He gave an almost imperceptible forward urge, and she stumbled on the curb. Like he had choreographed the whole deal, yeah, put him in charge of one of those Broadway losers, watch the money roll in. Quick as a flash, he steadied her with one hand, rubbed his chest against her shoulder blade, felt her stiffen at his uncomfortable closeness, the motion lifting her arms away from her sides, and he slid his free hand into her pocket.

Bummer. Nothing but a single card. Manny palmed the prize, switched to her other side. "Yeah, see, the Blades, they got the two blocks behind you, rule this world after dark. Goonies start the hospital's other side. Your workplace is sort of a no-man's-land, on account of half the guys are probably in there any given night. You know, gotta have a place to rest up and sharpen their knives."

He hustled her over a rough spot in the pavement, caught her with the tight-grip routine. "Watch it there. Street's like a battle zone, you know?" Another dip in the other pocket, second bummer of the day, nothing.

But Manny was nothing if not cool. Already he was working on who might buy a hospital ID. "There you go, pretty lady, all safe and sound, look, ready to go in there and save the world, am I right?"

"No, just one elderly lady," she said. "Only the true Lord can save us all."

"Hey, that's a good one. I gotta remember that." He released his grip, patted her arm. "You just watch it out here. The street's not nice to sweet little blond foreign girlies, you hear what I'm saying? Stay cool now."

Manny did his best strut around the corner, head cocked back, arms slack and body swinging, loose and limber and ready to bolt if she checked and realized he had dipped her pocket.

Not a peep.

Then the impossible happened. As he approached the far corner and safety, Manny broke one of his cardinal rules. He turned and looked back.

The foreign candy striper was still standing on the curb, watching him. At that moment, a sudden shaft of light split the cloudy gloom and landed upon her white-gold hair. For a moment, a bright arc shimmered over her head. She smiled and waved in his direction. Her smile was as pure as the light.

Manny then broke a second rule. He stopped. It was not a conscious act. His legs simply ceased to carry him forward. He stood there staring back and felt a hollow yearning blossom in the center of his chest. He lifted a feeble hand, drawn upward almost against his will, pulled by the same power that also pressed him to turn around, go back, confess his deed, give back the card. For a brief instant he was held there, feeling as though the light that shimmered about her reached out, farther and farther, enveloping him as well, offering a sense of devastatingly simple peace so powerful it shattered his world.

In a panic, Manny broke free and forced his shaky legs to carry him around the corner and away.

*M*anny ran for a time, not really seeing where he was going, too fractured internally to care. His streetwise front was cracked open, the lies of his life lying exposed. The air was suddenly so stifling that each breath threatened to puncture his lungs from within. He stopped and leaned against a wall, his chest heaving, and struggled to put his world back together again.

He found himself growing angry, battling against the invisible, twisting the memory of what happened to suit his own self-image, using rage as the glue to repair this upside-down perspective.

It was her looks. Yeah, had to be. Crazy that he'd let some wide-eyed pigeon get to him like that. Nuts. The street was gonna chew her up and spit her out. Serve her right, too. Shoulda stayed in the old country and sung to her cows or whatever it was that wide-eyed foreign pigeons did for fun. Manny pushed

himself erect, pulled his collar straight, slicked back his hair, willed his hands to stop shaking. No question, he was headed for the hot spots tonight. He needed to get his head straight, talk the stuff with some chickies who knew the score. Yeah, a major need.

The card. It was only then that he remembered he still had her card. He reached in his pocket, realized that he had already broken the third cardinal rule that day by not heading straight to his friendly neighborhood fence. One of the reasons Manny had never been caught was that he never held on to the goods for an instant longer than was necessary.

He pulled out the card, widened his eyes at the sight of his own reflection in the polished surface. He had never seen anything like it. Looked like it was made of sterling silver, only it was too light, weighed almost nothing. Felt like he was holding air. Manny turned it over, searched for markings, found none. Then he remembered an overheard conversation about some new cards in the making, smart cards they were called, couldn't be used by anybody but the owner, took a second ID or fingerprint to activate. Yeah, that was it. He'd heard they were already being used overseas.

Manny snorted his disgust. All shook up over a pigeon, and the only thing scored was a worthless card. He'd been taken good.

He was about to dump it when he passed a bank-in-the-box. He hesitated, then decided, why not? Might as well go for broke, give it a shot. He waited until the street was relatively clear, stepped forward, raised the card, scanned the street once more, then slid it into the slot.

There were none of the normal whirring, clattering sounds. Manny stiffened as a humming grew, his internal ears already hearing the sirens and the whooping alarm and the police whistles. Then the humming broke into a clarion trumpeting so loud and powerful and crystal clear that it froze him solid. There was no alarm to the sound, only power. It did not frighten. It *beckoned*. Manny stood in wide-eyed wonder and watched as the machine's edges began to shimmer. The shimmering grew brighter and brighter and brighter until he could no longer see the machine itself, nor the street, nor anything except that incredible silver-white light that reached out now, farther and farther, drawing him into the tunnel of brightness that had suddenly appeared where the machine had been. Pulling him in and sweeping him along, faster and faster and faster.

*E*xcuse me," she said hesitantly, leaning over the grimy counter.

"Yeah, what is it?" The balding, over-weight officer was too busy with his pile of papers and wad of gum to look up.

"I was told that you could help me."

A fleshy head lifted to fasten her with a stony gaze. A flicker of interest over the white-blond hair, the fresh face, the uniform, then dismissal. "So what's the problem?"

"I was," she stumbled over the word the woman who directed her to the desk had used, "pickpocketed."

"Hang on." He reached to one side,

plucked a sheet from one of perhaps a dozen tall piles. "You a foreigner?"

"Yes," she said, more definite this time.

"Thought so. Where's home?"

"Heaven."

"Never heard of it." He tested the pen on his thumb, bent over the form. "Okay, name?"

"Ariel."

"First or last?"

"Ah, first."

"Last?"

She was silent a moment, then, "Messenger."

"Address?"

"I'm just here." She waved her hand toward the door. "At the Providence General Hospital."

"That'll do for now." He scribbled down the words. "Okay, what'd you lose?"

"My pass."

"Train, subway, what?"

"No," again the stumble, then, "higher."

"Higher? Oh, right. Your plane ticket home. What about money, jewels, credit cards?"

"No, just my pass."

He stopped writing. "Were you mugged?"

"I'm sorry, I—"

"Attacked," he said impatiently, glancing at the line forming behind her. "Hit, slapped around, that sort of thing?"

A shudder ran through her body. "No, nothing like that. I don't even know who did it."

"A pro," said a voice behind her. She turned, saw a heavyset woman with eyes of eternal weariness seated on a bench alongside the wall. "Nice to see somebody taking pride in their work."

"You're lucky, honey," said the grimy man sprawled next to her. "Most of the jokers out there hit first, search later."

"But it's my pass home," Ariel said fearfully.

The police officer asked impatiently, "Does this pass have your name on it?"

"No," she replied sorrowfully. "I was warned not to lose it."

"Sounds like good advice to me. You shoulda listened better." The police officer tossed her form in the wastebasket at his feet. "Next."

"Come on, sister, move aside." A young man with a fishnet T-shirt and skintight jeans weaseled up. "You're not the only one's got problems."

"Tell me about it," the police officer said, his voice eternally bored. "Okay, so what's your beef?"

A hand tugged at Ariel's elbow. "I'm sorry, I couldn't help but hear." Bright eyes peered at her from beneath a stiff navy-blue cap, one quite different from those worn by the police surrounding them. Her blue uniform had emblems on each lapel which Ariel immediately recognized. "I'm Sister Clarice. What seems to be the problem?"

"I was supposed to just go in and see someone at the hospital and leave," Ariel said. "But now I've lost my pass and I can't get home."

The woman showed genuine sympathy as she asked, "They took all you had?"

"Everything," Ariel said sorrowfully.

The little woman *tch-tch*ed. "And now you don't have any place to stay?"

Ariel shook her head. "This was not supposed to happen."

Sister Clarice had a good chuckle over that. "Well, honey," she said, "that's life. Why don't you come with me, now, and I'll see if I can't find you a nice cup of tea."

"No, thank you, I—" She looked back over

at the desk sergeant. "Oh dear."

"What is it?"

Ariel sighed. "I haven't even seen to my task at the hospital."

"Well, of course, go get your work done, and I'll just finish handing out these tracts. Then when you're done, come meet me at the Salvation Army hall. You can't miss it, the big red brick building just opposite the hospital's main entrance."

*T*he hospital was busy and noisy and full of people tensely intent on their duties. Ariel was directed down endless halls filled with patients in various stages of distress. A few doors from her destination she had to stop and lean against the wall, her heart was so full of

sorrow and compassion for those who sur-
rounded her.

The door to the room suddenly opened,
and a group of women emerged. The last one
turned and said with forced cheerfulness,
"We'll be back in time to pray with you before
breakfast."

"Thank you, sister," said a feeble voice
from within.

"Sleep well," the gray-headed woman said
briskly. She managed to keep her smile in
place until the door had shut behind her. Then
her chin trembled, and she accepted a friend's
steadying hand. "Oh, Gladys."

"Have faith," her friend urged.

"I try, I try, but it's so hard," the woman
whispered. "It tears at me to see my best friend
in all the world lying there in such pain."

"She feels that the Lord has heard our
prayers," another said, drawing close. "She is
so certain of it."

"But—"

"No buts," her friend said gently. "We're
here beside you, dear. Lean on us. All we can
do is be there for her, pray with her, give her
love, and ask that His will be done." The group
drew close around the woman, and together

they walked down the long hall.

Ariel collected herself and entered the room. "Hello," she said softly.

"Oh, excuse me," the woman said, fumbling for her glasses. "I don't—"

"It's all right," Ariel said, drawing close enough to see that the woman's age-spotted cheeks were streaked with recent tears. She sat down on the edge of the bed and took the woman's free hand, willing love to flow between them. "It really is all right."

"My friends," the old woman said, and suddenly the tears started afresh. "They are all such good people."

"They love you very much," Ariel agreed.

The woman's tears continued. "I wouldn't mind going now, I really wouldn't. This old body is such a bother. But I keep having this *feeling*. I can't explain it better than that. It wakes me up at night. God is near, I know that with all my heart. I keep hoping He is here to guide me home. But then I have the feeling that my time has not yet come."

"No," Ariel agreed, and reached for the glass on the woman's bedside table. She unfastened the top button to her blouse, drew out the little satchel, and sprinkled a little of the sparkling powder into the water. Immediately the water began to shimmer with rainbow hues. "Would you like to drink this?"

"That's a strange place to be carrying medicine," the woman observed. "What is it?"

"I think you know," Ariel said quietly.

The woman glanced from the glass to Ariel's face and back again. Her eyes widened. "Are you—"

"Here," Ariel said softly. "A gift."

One trembly hand reached over and accepted the glass. The woman swallowed noisily, then lay back, tired from the effort. Ariel set down the glass, patted the woman's shoulder, and rose to her feet. "I must go."

"Wait," the woman said. She searched Ariel's face, then asked quietly, "What is it like?"

"Just as you said," Ariel replied, turning toward the door with a smile. "It is home."

*L*ight. Intensely glowing light. Issuing from everything. Light so softly powerful it was not content simply to shine upon him. Manny stood and felt the light illuminate the depths of his body and his mind.

Manny searched the chamber in which he stood, his heart pumping and his chest heaving like mad. The great room was empty save for the light that poured from every surface. White benches lined the featureless white walls. There was no nook, no cranny, no shadowy corner where he could flee and hide. He was totally and utterly exposed.

A door he had not seen slid back to admit a white-robed figure. Light shone from this person as well, making it hard for Manny to see whether it was man or woman, young or old.

The light-person turned and looked at him. Manny sought a frantic escape path, saw nothing, no way out, not even the door through which the person had entered. He could see nothing but the light.

A step closer, and Manny felt the light pouring forth with the person's gaze. It searched not his face, but rather his twisted spirit. The pain of being so exposed would have been unbearable had it not been for the love with which the person looked at him. It was unquestioning, given without measure, illuminating the empty depths within Manny and filling them to overflowing.

"You are not intended to be here," the person said.

"You're telling me," Manny stammered.

"You have something that is not yours. From whom did it come?"

Manny was about to break his last and final cardinal rule and tell the truth. But a lifetime of living on lies was a heavy chain that pulled at his soul. He opened and closed his mouth, doing his best imitation of a goldfish, immobilized by the love that threatened to melt him down and reform him totally. He could feel the love and the light withering away his life of lies, cauterizing the wounds he had inflicted on himself.

Then the pain of honest self-discovery

proved too much. Manny turned, and without another thought or instant of wondering what he was leaving behind, he spun on his heel and fled toward what appeared to be a featureless, light-filled wall.

A horn blared. Brakes squealed. Still blinded by what he had left behind, Manny leapt back and stumbled over the curb. A voice yelled out words which his mind could not yet take in, then the motor gunned and roared away.

He was back.

Manny raised himself up on trembling legs, dusted himself off, tried to still his heaving chest. His heart continued to beat like an overworked snare drum. He backed up to the wall, leaned heavy against it, tried to collect himself. He knew without understanding that the pain in his chest had nothing to do with his overworked heart. His whole being *ached* with a loss he could not fathom. He yearned for something he could scarcely believe existed.

The love. It lingered about him like the faintest perfume. The love and the light had *seared* him. In those few moments, he had felt as though unseen shadows had been stripped from his eyes, his mind, his body, his very life.

An empty, aching hollowness swelled within him, filled with the utter nothingness of a wasted life.

Then a lifetime of habits kicked in. Anger swelled to fill the empty void, and more lies formed to veil him from the truth. That was what he got for breaking his own rules. Nothing but trouble. He'd let himself go for one minute, let himself feel something for a pigeon, and what happened? He started slipping.

A two-minute flashback, yeah, that's what it was. Nothing but the dregs of a bad trip. Just forgetting who he was and what this world had in store for people who didn't keep it hard and sharp and fast and furious, letting a too-long night linger and let him go soft for some pigeon.

But it wouldn't happen again. Manny felt the anger mount, and used it to shove himself from the wall. He didn't just get by. He was a beast of the jungle. He fed on the prey. He was tough. He was a hunter.

Manny jerked his leather vest down straight, grabbed the silver card from the machine, turned down the side street, and eased into his familiar strut. A hunter, yeah.

That was the ticket. Remind himself of who he was and what he did. Then go out there and hunt down a few pigeons.

*T*he reed-thin old man standing guard at the Salvation Army's entrance gave her a smile of surprising brightness, considering his advanced years. "Can I help you, young lady?"

"I was looking for Sister Clarice."

"Sure, she told me to keep watch for a lost-looking foreign gal. Didn't say she'd light up the room with her looks, though." The old man cackled. "Shame I ain't ten years younger. Give those young boys a run for their money, I would."

"Stop with your jawing, already," com-

35

plained a derelict tottering two stairs below Ariel. "You're holding up traffic."

"Sorry, sorry." He urged Ariel over to one side. "Come right on in, ladies and gents. There's room for all. Same as the place awaiting you when all this is over."

"Yeah, right." A bitter-eyed young man stepped forward, held the door for a woman carrying a whimpering child. "You're gonna feed me the line about mansions in the sky, that it?"

"Don't aim on feeding you anything your heart ain't hungry for," the old man said easily. "But if you fill your belly and still find yourself empty, you can come back and we'll chat."

"I never had any idea the work was so hard," Ariel said softly, watching the young man take the child from his woman and walk toward the cafeteria line.

"Hard it is for anybody with eyes ready to see and a heart ready to feel," the old man said, but his eyes remained bright and his tone cheerful. "Only way to make it through the day is to remember who it is we're here to serve."

Ariel turned back to the old man, placed a gentle hand upon his arm. "You speak like one who knows the way home."

"Ariel, welcome, welcome." Sister Clarice came over, wiping her hands on her apron. "Did the police find your things?"

"No," Ariel said worriedly. "I don't know what to do."

"Well, nothing like a nice cup of tea to set the world straight, I always say." She steered Ariel into the hall. "Now, would you like to sit, or would you like to come chat with me while I serve? It's almost lunchtime, you see, and we'll soon be up to our ears with hungry people."

"Can I help?"

"Bless you, child, what a nice thing to hear. As a matter of fact, we're short one pair of hands. A volunteer hasn't shown up yet, and the line is due to open in just five minutes. If you wouldn't mind serving the soup, it would be a blessing."

"Of course."

"Wonderful, just wonderful. Here, take my apron so you don't dirty up that lovely uniform of yours. And if you could manage a smile and a nice word, these folks would be more than grateful. We try to show them that someone still cares for them, you see. You'll find that often means more to them than the food."

Sister Clarice made a series of swift introductions before stationing Ariel behind a great gleaming vat of soup. She stood and watched as more and more people filtered in through the door to be greeted cheerfully by the old man. Some responded with a grunt, some with anger, some with a yearning word or two that twisted her heart. Ariel stood and inspected the growing line of men and women and children, saw worry and desperation and hunger and fear and pain etched deep into their dirty, lined features. It was all she could do not to cry.

Sister Clarice noticed her distress and moved over. "Now, don't let it get to you," she warned. "Remember, we're not called to solve all the world's problems. We must simply do what we can with what we have."

Ariel nodded her understanding, yet felt the woman's words ringing inside her head. *What we have.*

She reached up and plucked the sachet from within her uniform, drawing it up and over her head. She glanced about, saw that everyone was busy with their last-minute duties, opened the little sack, and dumped the entire contents into the soup.

She bowed her head through the blessing, hoping that what she had done was acceptable, knowing that she could have done nothing else.

"My, my, that soup smells *good*." A smiling black face stood waiting in front of her when she opened her eyes. "How you doing, sister? Don't believe I've seen your pretty face around these parts before."

"This is Ariel," Sister Clarice said from farther down the line. "She's a new volunteer."

"Well, bless you, sister," the black man said. "Surely is nice to set eyes on a pretty young thing. You make that soup up special today?"

Ariel ladled out a bowl, handed it

39

over, replied, "Just added a little spice."

"I hear you," he said, moving on. His place was taken by a gray-bearded man whose grimy features were set in a permanently twisted scowl. Ariel smiled through the shared pain of what lay beneath the man's expression and handed over a bowl. On and on the procession went, each face holding a thousand stories. Ariel did as Sister Clarice had suggested, and shared from all she had.

*T*his diner served the worst coffee in all Philadelphia. Still, Manny spent a lot of time there, a cup resting untouched on the counter beside him. Through the steamy front window Manny could look across the street and survey the pawnshop's entrance. As usual, he had a system worked out.

Manny lived by his wits. Always had. He had fashioned a life based on speed and agility and freedom, his desire for close relationships quenched at an early age by a mother who drank and fathers who changed by the week. Schooling had ended the summer he had been dumped on the streets at the age of eleven. Manny had not minded so much. At least the current old man had given him time to get situated before winter hit.

And he'd done all right since then. A loner's loner, he had learned to skirt the city jungle shadows, ever wary of the bigger forces at work—the blue-clad soldiers and the beasts of the night. Both were eager to ensnare him, one to put him in a cage of steel, the other to make him their slave. Manny strived for invisibility and paid homage to none.

Now he sat watching the pawnshop with a stillness that would have surprised those who knew his quickness on the street. Watching and waiting. As always, he allowed a full ten minutes from the departure of the last customer, no matter how long it took, adding those who entered and subtracting all who left, making sure no surprise lay waiting for him in some unseen back room.

When the shop had stood silent and still for the prescribed time, Manny rose from his stool, paid for coffee he had not touched, left the diner, checked the street, crossed, checked again, and entered.

"Manny, hey, just the guy I was looking for." Spider was a bent, hairless man whose overly white limbs seemed to lack both joints and bones. He spent the better part of his life perched upon a stool from which he could survey his little kingdom. "Where you been keeping yourself?"

Manny's internal alarm started flashing. Spider was not a man known for his hospitality, especially to people trying to sell him something. "Same place as always, Spider. The streets."

"Yeah, I hear you." He shifted his stool closer to the wire cage through which he conducted all business and hit the unseen switch that locked the front door.

The first time he had done that, Manny had gone totally berserk. He had always harbored a grim terror of enclosed spaces. But Spider had soothed him, walked over, shown him how the door could now be opened only from within. A twist of the little lever, see, and Manny was free to go. The electric lock was for the special protection of his special clients.

Manny had fished up a sickly grin, wiped off the sweat, and gotten down to business. But he still hated the sound of that electric bolt snapping into place.

Spider slid a hand the color of a fish's belly through the little slit-opening at the base of his wire cage. Overlong fingers beckoned impatiently. "C'mon, Manny, let's see what you got for your friend Spider today."

Manny walked over, all his sensors on overdrive. This kind of eagerness was new. Spider always acted reluctant when it came to fencing goods, pulling these long faces and talking in mournful tones about how tight the market was for whatever Manny had brought in, dried up or flooded or just not there anymore, sorry, the best he could do would be five cents on the dollar, max.

Manny was used to playing the game. It was part of the price he paid for staying independent. He always entered the pawnshop knowing he was in for a hard-fought battle. But something was wrong now. Spider's new attitude left the hairs on the back of his neck standing on end.

"Got some top quality goods, Spider," he said, forcing himself to play it cool, strutting over, reaching for the hidden pockets in his vest and down inside his boot, all the while keeping one eye and an ear tuned for something, anything, either from behind the curtained back door or out front. Yeah, a single whisper of sound, a flicker of movement, one isolated footstep, and Manny would vanish like smoke in the wind. "Check this out, a gold Rolex. And a diamond bracelet, no less. Markings on the back are solid, I already checked. Platinum and fourteen carat."

"You're the best, Manny, the best, I always said it." Impatiently Spider shoved the items to one side. "What else you got?"

"Hey, hang on a sec, we're talking top drawer here." Manny risked a complete swivel, searched the street in both directions as far as he could see. Nothing. Not a movement, not even a car. Still the nerves in his gut jangled their constant warning. "Couldn't take less than an even thou."

"Right, right." The unseen drawer slid back, the roll was plucked out, impatient fingers counted to ten. "Thousand on the nose.

Just like you asked. I always treated you good, right, Manny? Always played it straight with my number-one man. Now what else you got?"

"What is this?" Manny asked, his heart rate soaring for the third time that day. "You setting me up, Spider?"

"Me?" A bead of perspiration dribbled down from his hairless temple, across the skin of a cheek that had not felt the sunlight in years. "There ain't no future in that. Why'd I want to do in my number-one source of prime goods?"

"Something ain't right," Manny muttered and crept to the door. He sprang the catch, swung the door wide, searched the empty street, then slammed down the rubber doorstop. "We'll finish our business with the door open, that all right with you?"

"Open, closed, what difference does it make to me? Only reason I lock it is for your protection, you know that, Manny."

"Right. Then you won't mind if I just check out back." Without waiting for a reply, Manny walked over and pushed open the back door hard enough to flatten anyone waiting on the other side. He searched the back hall, found

45

nothing but dust and stale odors.

"You satisfied now? Can we get down to it?"

"Yeah, guess so." Manny walked back and squinted at the white-faced man with undisguised hostility. "Why are you sweating, Spider?"

"Who wouldn't be, the way you're acting." The shoulderless man raised one limp hand and swiped at the sweat that glistened on his upper lip. "Now c'mon, Manny, let's see the rest."

"An alligator wallet, a dozen credit cards, a pocket watch, that's the lot," Manny said, handing over the goods while keeping his attention on the front door. All he wanted was to be away.

Frantic fingers flipped through the credit cards, opened the wallet, searched all the pockets, then the tightening voice croaked, "It ain't there!"

Manny swung back. "What're you talking about?"

"Didn't you get something else today, Manny? Think hard, big guy. Anything else you wanna show your old buddy Spider?"

Manny squinted through the wire cage.

The pale-white man was sweating fiercely now. "Like what?"

"Anything, you know, like maybe something you forgot, maybe you slipped into another pocket, you know. Maybe a card or something."

"Give me the money," Manny hissed.

Spider peeled the bills off the roll with hands that moved with the desperate motions of two frightened animals. "Hey, sure, but look, don't you want to just check, you know, look through your pockets, maybe one more time for old Spider, you know, just to make sure?"

"That's all there is," Manny said, shoveling the money into his pocket without counting.

"Look, hey, you're my main guy, right? Don't you just want to—"

Manny gripped the wire. "Who's been following me, Spider?"

"Nobody, hey, c'mon, what is this—"

"What else am I supposed to have, then?"

"Look, hey, it's no big deal. Just a card, maybe a little different, I dunno, silver kinda." Both hands wiped down a sweat-drenched face. "I just heard, you know, maybe you'd gotten hold of this card."

47

"From who?" Manny growled, feeling the walls closing in, wanting to flee, but needing to know who was dogging his steps.

"You don't want to know." The white face turned even paler, the colorless eyes opened wider. "Believe me, big guy, it ain't in your best interest. You'll live longer."

"Tell me," Manny demanded.

"Look, I can't, really. But if you've got anything like what they want, then you'd better let me have it. I mean, it's just a card, right?"

"See you, Spider," Manny said, turning away.

"Manny, wait!" Panic raised the man's voice an octave. "These guys, they ain't the kind you want to tangle with, you know what I mean? Manny, don't go, hey, it ain't smart—"

Manny hit the sidewalk already powering toward liftoff, his eyes searching every nook and cranny and shadow, seeing nothing, yet feeling eyes follow him everywhere. Evil eyes. Eyes that promised nothing but menace and terror.

*I*t was raining hard the next morning. Ariel had never imagined that such rain could exist. All the trees she could see through the little kitchen window were bowed and shaking, their lower limbs so wind-tossed they scraped the ground, back and forth, shivering and heavy and wishing for a way out of the cold storm.

Which was exactly the way Ariel felt, too.

"Oh, good morning, dear." Sister Clarice tottered in, looking decidedly older and more frail in her pink bathrobe than she had the day before when wearing her blue uniform. "Have you been up long?"

"No." Ariel sighed and turned away from the window. No answers there. No answers anywhere, as far as she could tell. "Thank you so much for bringing me home last night."

"Oh, my dear." Sister Clarice came around and patted her hand. "You looked so lost and so worried, how could I not help?"

49

The kindness in the woman's touch and the warmth in her eyes gave Ariel such a powerful feeling of home that she felt a burning misery collect in her eyes. She was indeed lost.

"Now, now," Clarice murmured. "Why don't you just come right over here and sit down at the table while I make us both a nice cup of tea. Would you like some toast and honey for breakfast?"

"I don't know," she replied honestly.

"Well, I've always said when the mind is too busy worrying to be hungry, that's usually when the body could do with a good feeding."

Sister Clarice bustled about, filling a pot and placing it on the stove, then cutting bread with a long serrated knife. Ariel watched her deft motions and asked, "Have you ever been worried?"

Clarice laughed so hard she had to set down the knife and hold the kitchen cabinet with both hands. "How on earth do you think I earned all these wrinkles? Each and every one is a graduation present from the school of hard knocks."

"I don't think I've ever heard of that place."

"Then you are one lucky young woman."

She popped two pieces into the toaster. "Bet you've never had homemade bread before either."

"Never," Ariel agreed.

"Child, this world has a way of surprising us almost every day. Some of these surprises

are so good they make us want to shout to the heavens with joy. Others, well, the best thing we can say is that these too shall pass. And why can you always say that for certain?" Clarice picked up the whistling pot and answered her own question as she poured water into two cups. "Because this is not our home."

"I know," Ariel said softly.

"Of course you do. The first time I saw you I said to myself, now there is the face of a believer." Clarice set a steaming cup in front of Ariel. "Then you should know that no matter what you are facing, you must remain stead-fast in your faith, and pray."

"Pray," Ariel repeated faintly.

"That's right. Pray with all your might. Pray without ceasing. Pray for guidance, pray for strength, pray for wisdom. And one day you will hear the Lord's clarion call, and the angels will lift you from this vale of trials and temptations, and carry you to where you will never worry again. Not ever."

"I wish that were true," Ariel said, her voice very quiet.

Instead of answering sharply, Clarice inspected Ariel's face. "Is it truly that bad, child?"

"Terrible," Ariel replied and felt the sud-den burning return to her eyes.

"Do you want to tell me about it?"

She thought it over, then said doubtfully,

"I'm not sure that I can."

"Well, if you ever feel the need to unburden, I've been called a fair listener in my day."

"Thank you," Ariel said. "You are a friend."

Clarice beamed at that, then continued to bustle about the little kitchen, setting down toast and butter and honey. "Now you just put your mind at ease about one thing. You can stay here as long as you like. In the meantime, though, I need to help with a new church project. It will take me to Washington, but I'll only be gone three or four—"

"Washington!" Ariel brightened. "I know that name."

"That's our nation's capital, dear." Clarice looked more closely at the young woman seated across from her. "Where was it that you said you were from?"

"I have a friend there. I think I do. I think she said she needed to stay longer. Miss . . ." Ariel scrunched up her forehead in concentration, then remembered. "Simpkins! Yes, I'm sure that's right. And she was working at a hospital just like me." The pretty forehead scrunched up again. "But what was the hospital's name?"

"And can she help you with your problem?"

"Oh yes," Ariel said, more certain than she had been all morning. "I'm sure she can."

"Well, that settles it then." Clarice set one firm hand on the tabletop. "You'll just have to come with me."

"Oh, could I?"

"I don't suppose you have any money, do you? No, it would all have been taken by the pickpocket." Clarice did some swift calculations. "I think I have enough for two tickets. I'm afraid we'll be traveling rather rough, though. I don't have much extra to my name." She looked at her watch and rose from the table. "If we're going, we'll have to start now. The bus leaves in less than an hour. Come along, my dear. Let us see if you can fit into any of my clothes."

I tell you, I have been visited by an angel!"

Manny froze at the words. He had been searching the hospital corridors for some sign of the young woman, not sure what he was going to do if he found her, but knowing he had to look just the same. He had found nothing at all and was heading back down toward the entrance, wondering at his next step, when he heard the old lady's proclamation.

"I'm sure she was, mother," said a younger woman, her tone oozing false comfort. "Now, why don't you just lie back and let's wait for the doctor."

Manny hung back around the corner, pretending to read down a list of doctors' names and office numbers, his attention remaining focused on the conversation in the next room. Actually, it was more like an argument, except that the couple in the old lady's room were too polite to actually say in words what they

55

thought, so they said it with the tone of their voices. And what they thought was that the old lady was making about as much sense as a loon.

Only Manny was beginning to think differently.

"I tell you, I don't *want* to lie back down." The old lady was beginning to grow angry. "Has this visitation robbed me of my ability to speak clear English? Listen to what I am saying, daughter. I am *healed*."

"Now, mother—"

"Oh, let her get out of bed if she wants to," said an impatient male voice, one filled with the weight of his own importance. "Then we can help her up off the floor and maybe have some peace around here for a change."

"You're a fat lot of help," the young woman snapped.

"All I said was—"

"Oh, go see what's holding up that blasted doctor, why don't you?" And then back to the wheedling tone: "Now, Mom, let me just—"

"Keep your distance, daughter. I'm in no mood for any of your mollycoddling."

A starched figure strode impatiently past Manny, scarcely noticing him as he swept around the corner and into the room. "Oh, good. You're all together. Right. Well. I honestly don't know how to put this to you folks, but there appears to be a complete and total remission."

There was a stunned silence, followed by the young man's demanding, "Just exactly what are you saying, doctor?"

"What I am saying," the physician replied, "is that I can find no indication of your mother's illness. Not a trace. Not anywhere."

"Then do some more tests," the young woman insisted.

"I have already done every test known to science," the doctor replied. "Twice. And I am telling you that your mother appears to be completely healed."

"I could have told you that and saved everybody a lot of bother," the old lady retorted.

"But you said—"

"I know what I said," the doctor butted in. "And these test results fly completely in the face of modern medicine. But there you are."

The silence descended once more. Finally the young woman said in a numb voice, "I don't know what to think."

"Well I do," the old lady said. "If you people will kindly step outside for a moment, I am going to put on my clothes and get home just as fast as these old legs will carry me."

"Mother—"

"You heard me. Now scat."

Manny took a few steps toward the elevator as the trio emerged and walked past him, the couple too deep in discussion with the doctor to pay him any mind. He waited as long as he dared, fearing that the daughter would return at any moment, then retraced his steps and knocked softly on the door.

"If that's you, daughter," came the muffled reply, "you are about to get a piece of my mind."

"It's not her," Manny said. "Can I come in?"

"No, wait, just a minute. All right." The door opened to reveal a seamed face with brightly inquisitive eyes. "You're not with the hospital staff."

"No, I'm . . ." Manny stopped. Who was he? "I'm looking for someone."

"There's nobody in here but me."

"No, wait, I, well, I was looking for a girl."

"Ah." The gaze focused in more tightly. "You saw her too, did you?"

58

"I'm not sure," Manny said, feeling some-how defeated. "Maybe. No, probably."

"I wasn't sure either until the miracle opened my eyes." The woman pushed the door open wide, searched the corridor, asked, "Have you seen that daughter of mine?"

"I think she left with the doctor."

"She's a wonderful child, but unfortunately she inherited her father's bullheadedness, God rest his stubborn soul. Once she gets an idea into her head, you need a blowtorch and a bull-dozer to shift it." She turned back and walked to her closet. "Come in, young man."

He crept into the room. "What did she look like, the girl you met?"

"Girl, woman, angel, who knows the right word." She offered him her coat. "Would you be a gentleman and help me on with this?"

"Uh, sure."

"Thank you. Well, what I saw at first was a young girl with hair the color of sun-ripened corn and eyes like an early summer sky. So open and trusting you would have thought she had been raised in a convent."

Manny remembered the way she had looked at him, with a gaze so clear he felt as though he could hold her heart in his hands.

Then he remembered how he had acted and what he had said, and suddenly he felt dirtier than he had ever felt in his entire life. "That's her," he mumbled.

"Yes. But afterward . . ." The old lady buttoned up her coat and turned, her face glowing as she looked at him. "After the miracle, I could only remember her, you see, because she had already left. But I knew. Oh my, yes, there wasn't any room for doubt then. God had heard my prayer, and He had sent me an angel of mercy."

Mercy. He felt stabbed by the power of a word he scarcely knew the meaning of. "Do you know where she went?"

"Back home, I suppose." The old lady patted his arm. "My advice to you, young man, is to pray to God. If you pray hard and long, He will hear. Whether or not He will send you an angel, I can't say. But He will hear. And He will answer. Of that you can rest assured."

*T*he Philadelphia bus station is not a very
pleasant place," Clarice said apologetically.
"But I'm afraid it's all I can afford."

Ariel stood at Clarice's side, moving in
step with her as the ticket line inched forward.
She did not know where to look in the station.
The once grand structure had been reduced to
an echoing den of noise and confusion and dirt
and squalor. Several of the hard central seats
were occupied by homeless people, slumped
over in exhausted or drugged slumber.
Around them, groups of young men played
games that truly frightened Ariel, though she
did not understand why.

The men hovered by each arriving bus,
smiling with the bottom halves of their faces,
their eyes hidden behind ultra-dark sunglasses.
To young alighting passengers they would
speak words Ariel could not hear and did not
want to, then turn and squabble with other
men trying to do the same thing. Jostling each

other with fury and threats while trying to hold to smiles for the teenaged travelers who walked through the doors with faces full of anxiety and expectation. The game had an insane quality to it, one which left Ariel feeling as though she stood at the edge of a precipice.

When Clarice had paid for their two tickets and turned away from the counter, Ariel pointed and asked, "What is that all about?"

"Those are runaways, dear." She picked up her suitcase and started away. "Come, our bus leaves in fifteen minutes."

Ariel picked up the small cardboard and vinyl case that Clarice had lent her and hurried to catch up. She walked a little clumsily in Clarice's skirt, which was folded back over itself and pinned at her side in order to make it fit. She also wore a simple white blouse and fuzzy pink sweater, all from Clarice's drawer. "What is a . . .what you said?"

"A runaway," Clarice repeated patiently. "They leave their homes, some for good reasons and some for no reasons at all. They take buses to the big city, and people like these men you see here try to take them and use them."

Ariel's gaze shifted from the charade to Clarice and back again. "Use them for what?"

"If you don't know," Clarice replied, "I advise you not to ask. Now come along, dear. We must hurry."

As they walked down the long foyer with its line of doors leading to the bus platforms, Clarice went on, "The organization I belong to, The Salvation Army, is a special kind of church. We work with the lost, the helpless, the hopeless, the homeless. We serve the ones who are forgotten by society. There you can see some of our young members trying to steer these runaways away from the chasm."

The chasm. Ariel saw four men wearing ties and kind faces, men strong enough to deter the gangs from trying to shove them out, standing by a placard that read, "Free food, free rest, free hope." A pair of young girls stood in front of them, tattered backpacks at their feet. They looked very tired and very frightened. Just out of reach, young men gathered and taunted the group.

When Clarice tried to walk between the Salvation Army stand and the group of hovering young men, one of them bounced her with his hip, causing her to stumble into Ariel. "Watch out where you're going, gramma."

"Vultures, that's what you are," Clarice

retorted. "All of you."

"Hey, get a load of the goods," said another, pointing at Ariel. "C'mon, sweet thing. For you we got a surprise. And you're just gonna love it."

Ariel stared at the young men. She could not help it. There was such a bizarre strangeness to them, such a total absence of everything she had thought of as constant, permanent, eternal.

"Come along, dear," Clarice said. "We mustn't miss our bus."

Ariel looked at the woman but did not move. There was such strength in the little lady's voice. How could she not be shaken by such strangeness? She turned back to the taunter, saw the tension and the anger and the chasm that separated them from eternity. *What am I to do?* she cried silently.

The call lofted upward, and returned to her with reassuring calm. She felt a power sweep through her. It showed through her gaze, communicating with a force beyond words. She stared at the young man until he and his mates were stilled.

Ariel spoke then, and it seemed that another voice spoke through her. A voice so silent that only the heart could hear, yet mighty enough to shatter the youth's cloak of lies. She said, "It is still not too late for you. But it soon will be."

"Watch out, man, she's givin' you the evil eye." But the taunt fell as flat as the young man's tone, drained of energy by what he faced.

Ariel stood and searched each face in turn. The power filling her gave her an ability to see shadows hovering about the young men. With their black sunglasses and black T-shirts and jeans, and with the shadows surrounding them, the youths looked like dark and hungry birds of prey.

Yet even here she saw hope. The Spirit's power sought not to condemn, but to *invite.* "Turn away," she pressed quietly. "Turn away from your evil deeds and thoughts, and hear the Lord's call. It is your only chance."

The moment remained frozen and apart from the swirling throng. The young men stood slack-jawed, silent, trapped by the power that flowed from her. Then one of them shuddered and straightened and dismissed her with a contemptuous wave. "Aw, she's just another one of them religious twits." He dug an elbow into the ribs of his nearest companion. "Come on, let's get out of here. Too much of that stuff'll drive you nuts."

The young men dispersed, the scene melted back into the noisy tumult of the station, and Clarice touched her arm. "We must hurry," she said, a trace of new respect to her voice. "Or we'll miss our bus."

*C*an I help you, son?"

"Yeah, uh, maybe." Manny was not used to politeness. Nor smiles. Not like this. Not open and welcoming. Especially not from a stranger standing in a doorway in this part of town. "I was just looking for somebody."

"Well, come in, come in. Everybody is

welcome here, no matter what the reason. We don't turn anybody away as long as there's room. Are you hungry?"

"Yeah, I guess."

"Step right this way, then." The old man moved with the unsteady steps of a dedicated alcoholic, but his eyes and his speech held the clarity of one long sober. He led Manny through the long chamber, where half-filled trestle tables lined a scuffed and ancient floor. At the far end stood a stage and podium and a half-circle of seats. Beyond that rose a simple wooden cross. The opposite corner opened into a kitchen alcove, fronted by a line of women serving food. They were smiling too. "Just grab a tray there, and take what you like."

"Sandra, this young man says he's come looking for somebody, but he decided he was hungry too." The old man patted Manny's arm and turned away. "Just tell this gal your troubles, son. She'll take care of you."

"Hello there." Sandra was so thin her clothes appeared to weigh more than she did. But her eyes were kind, and her smile came straight from the heart. "Who was it you wanted to find?"

"A girl," he said. "I don't know if she was

here. But a guard at the hospital entrance said he thought he saw her come in here. She's, uh, about this tall, blond, wore one of them hospital uniforms, looked like a candy-cane with starch, and—"

"Ariel!" Sandra cried. At the sound of that name all eyes turned their way. Sandra looked toward the kitchen and said, "This young man is looking for Ariel!"

Ariel. For reasons he could not understand, Manny felt a sudden thrill. He had a name for the girl now. Ariel.

A trio of smiling faces appeared from the cooking steam. "Ain't she just an angel?" one purred.

"Never saw nobody able to lift a body's spirits like that girl," chimed in another.

"An angel," Manny muttered. "Right."

"How do you know her, what did you say your name was?"

"From the street," he replied. That didn't sound too good, so he added, "And the hospital. Sort of."

"That girl was just heaven-sent," sighed the third woman. "Why, that very same day she was in here helping us, we had the most wonderful experience."

"Still can't hardly believe it, and I was there," agreed the first woman.

"We know lots of sad cases here," Sandra said, picking up the story. "It comes with the territory, I suppose. But that day, when was it, my goodness, it was only yesterday. Seems like years ago. Anyway, Ariel was standing right here beside me, when suddenly one of the people she was serving started to laugh. I mean, we hear lots of sounds in here, but we don't get laughs all that often—at least not this kind of laugh. It was just the happiest sound, and then some of the children started to sing, and Ariel joined in, my goodness, you shoulda heard that girl's voice. What was it she sang?"

"It was a hymn," another said. "I don't remember which. But pretty soon the whole hall was standing and holding hands and singing and laughing and praising God, good gracious me, I don't think I'll ever forget that as long as I live."

"Strange how I can't remember what it was we were singing," the first one mused. "I stood right there and sang for what seemed like hours. Serving folks and laughing with the children and singing my heart out. And now I can't remember—"

"Anyway," said the third woman, "Ariel went home with Sister Clarice. Seems the poor girl is from somewhere out of town and didn't have any place to stay."

"Out of town," Manny said. "Right."

"Sister Clarice won't be in today," Sandra said apologetically. "She had to go on a little trip, but she'll be back in a few days. Why don't you stop by again. I'm sure she would love to speak with you, especially if you're a friend of Ariel's."

*H*ey, Manny, long time no see." The young man motioned tersely with his head toward the empty stool beside him. As Manny seated himself, the guy drained his glass, asked, "What's going down?"

"Not much." Manny took in the long row of empty shot glasses in front of the man. "You keeping score?"

"Oblivion, Manny." The guy set the glass carefully into line, tapping the bottom on the bar in signal for another. "Tonight I am headed for the abyss, and I want to see how much it takes to get me there."

Needles. That was the guy's name. Manny had scored a couple of times with him, talked to him on a few other occasions, but he was like a hundred other guys in seedy dives. The names were nothing but labels. They easily melded into one another.

Manny felt the violence simmering under the young man's taut surface, knew with such an intake it could erupt at any time. Still, he felt drawn to the spot, and for the life of him could not understand why. He sighed in defeat and signaled the bartender. "Mind if I join you?"

"Help yourself. There's room for everybody where I'm headed." The guy suddenly found that hilarious and took his laughter with him as he raised his head and drained another glass.

Manny hunched over his drink and the

sodden bar, wishing he were somewhere else. This was definitely not his scene. A darkened dive on the corner of gang turf, most of the patrons either underage gang members or bikers, all of them ready to use any excuse or none at all to prove they were tough enough to survive in the jungle they called home ground.

He had headed back toward his apartment from the Salvation Army shelter, frustrated that his search had dead-ended, confused that he was searching at all. There was no reason, no explaining what kept driving him from one uncomfortable situation to another. An angel. It was crazy. The whole thing was nuts. But still there was something, some inner aching, twisting emptiness that just would not let go.

And now this. He had passed the bar as he always did, walking on the other side of the street and going as fast as he could without running. Gang turf was dangerous terrain these days, what with the druggies and the schizos and the young kids looking to earn their rank. But something had made him stop. And then turn and cross the street, despite the fact that his mind kept screaming danger. Crazy. Manny only went into a gang bar on business. But here he was. His feet had drawn him toward the door almost as though he had had no say in the matter.

Needles drained another glass, lined it up, tapped the bar, said without looking up, "Salerno's looking for fresh meat."

That was nothing new. Salerno ran houses from here to Vegas. Manny took a cautious sip, checked the bar for danger, felt it everywhere. "So?"

"So me and some of the guys, we were down at the station today. Playing keepers of the gate, you know, talking trash with the babes."

Manny knew. Places like bus stations and video arcades and downtown burger joints were called gateways. Gangs used them to gather up the unwary, boys and girls alike, and steal them away. Most were never heard from again.

"The religious wackos were there with the sign and the ties and everything." Another drink, another tap, another glass lined up. Still his voice remained taut, the words clear, as though something was keeping him wound up so tight the alcohol couldn't do its work. "Got between us and a couple of babes. Nice ones."

Manny started to draw away, sensing the

buildup of tension. But something held him there, an invisible hand that settled him in his seat, clamped him in place, kept him listening.

"Then there was this old lady. Don't ask me where she came from 'cause I don't know. And another babe. Nice. But dressed silly. Big old sweater, flapping dress, white shoes like you see on a nurse."

Now it was Manny who tensed. "Blond hair?"

"Yeah, real nice, like I said, even if she did dress like a bag lady." Another glass drained, another tap. "So we start on her and the old lady, you know, shoot her the line. And then she turns on me, and man, it was just weird. Like something outta the Twilight Zone. I mean, a real witch. I swear that woman put a spell on me or something."

Manny turned around in his stool, leaned his elbows on the bar, too anxious to hold still. Yet the invisible hand did not let him go. He sat there, wondering at how it was possible to be where he was and feel *led*. Like there was something or someone there with him, directing him forward. "You didn't see where they were headed, did you?"

"Got on the Washington bus, I know on

account of I was still watching 'em." Another glass, another tap, a shake of the head. "Ambushed. Trapped in her spell. Awful, Manny. A nightmare."

Manny sat and listened and looked out over the scene. Suddenly he felt a chill spread through his frame. In the distant corner the dark shadows seemed to shift. At first he thought it was a trick of the dim lights, but then he felt the invisible hand abruptly release him. Suddenly Manny sensed he was seeing something that had always been there, a threat that knew him and followed him and *wanted* him.

"Gotta go," Manny said, sliding from the stool. "Take it easy, Needles."

"Had to be a witch," the guy muttered, not looking up from his glass. "Caught me in a spell. Won't let me go."

"Clarice, over here! Hello, hello, how wonderful to see you again." The handsome man wore an elegantly cut dark suit with a gray silk tie to match his hair. A gold cross sparkled on his lapel. "I do so wish you would have let me fly you down."

"Nonsense. Especially when the bus station is only blocks from your church. How are you, Leslie?"

"Fine, fine. Better when we're away from here." The elegant man was clearly ill at ease with his surroundings. He led them down the outer sidewalk, skirting around the worst of the bus station's evening crowd. "We may be only blocks away from the White House, as the tourist brochures say, but we are also only blocks from some of the nation's most dangerous neighborhoods."

"Which is why I am here," Clarice replied primly, not the least disturbed by the cacophony they passed.

"Indeed, yes. Let me take your case. This way, please." Then he noticed Ariel walking close to Clarice. He started to stop for introductions, but his sense of self-preservation overcame his natural politeness, and he made do with asking over his shoulder, "Who do we have here?"

"This is Ariel," Clarice replied. "She is staying with me for a few days from . . ." She turned a questioning gaze toward her companion.

"Far away," Ariel replied vaguely, her attention captured by the spectacle. She stared at a scene almost identical to the one she had left in Philadelphia, the same noise and tumult and anger and danger. Two stations, anchors of darkness at either end of such a pleasant journey. Like so much of what she had seen since her arrival. So much beauty and so much sadness, all mixed and tangled so tightly she could not look for one without finding the other. "Very far away," she murmured.

"This is Reverend Leslie Townsend," Clarice said. To Townsend she explained, "Ariel stopped by our center yesterday. Her first day on the job at the hospital, and wouldn't you know it, she was robbed. Lost everything she owned, cash, identity papers, everything except the uniform she was wearing. Isn't that right, dear?"

"Everything," Ariel agreed.

"How terrible," the pastor said, and pointed ahead. "There's our car. I had to bring Hale, my assistant, with me to watch the car. Otherwise we would have found ourselves walking back. Not something you want to do around here, I assure you."

"Leslie's church is one of the oldest in Washington," Clarice told Ariel. "A very beautiful place, although the neighborhood around it has deteriorated considerably. Instead of ignoring the difficulties around them, they have decided to set up a soup kitchen and homeless center."

"And a day-care center for the children," the pastor added, stopping by the car and popping the trunk. "Not to mention a group that plans to minister in this very bus station starting tomorrow. But only after years and years of turning the blind eye, I am ashamed to say."

"Well, at least you are helping now," Clarice corrected him, smiling at a young black man who had emerged from the front seat.

"That is more than most. And from what I
hear, you had to go through quite a struggle to
get this far."

"Yes, there was a lot of resistance,"
Townsend agreed, and for a moment his handsome face showed the strain and the fatigue.
"But thanks to people like Hale and some in
the congregation who felt called to help, we
are finally underway. Which is why we are so
grateful that you would come down and
advise us."

"Anything I can do to help," Clarice
replied. She shook Hale's hand, introduced
Ariel, and allowed herself to be seated in the
backseat.

"If you don't mind," Leslie said, sliding in
behind the wheel, "I'll take you directly to the
church. We have a regular church gathering
this evening. It started as a small Bible study
and prayer meeting, but my goodness, you
would not believe how it has grown."

"Almost fills the nave," Hale agreed. He
had a voice as mild as his eyes, in direct con-
trast to the strength radiating from his face.
"All in the space of three months."

"Hale and I take turns leading the service,"
Leslie went on. "Oh, by the way, I don't sup-

pose you play a musical instrument."

Clarice laughed. "Oh, not me. I couldn't carry a tune in a bucket. When it comes to music, my job on earth is to be a good listener." She looked at Ariel. "What about you, dear?"

Ariel shrugged, her face turned to the window. So much to see, so much to take in, all of it new. "Just the harp."

"The harp!" Leslie and Hale exclaimed together. Leslie went on, "That is amazing."

"A miracle," Hale agreed.

"We like to have guest musicians at these evening get-togethers," Leslie explained. "We had a harpist who was supposed to play tonight, but he's come down with the flu. We just got the call as we were walking out the door to come pick you up."

"So now we've got this huge harp sitting in the middle of our nave, with nobody to play it." Hale turned in his seat. "I don't suppose you would be willing to help us out tonight, would you?"

anny stumbled up the stairs, not from fatigue, but rather from a sense that he should be doing something else. First this had made him mad, then it made him stubborn. Manny hated having someone tell him what to do. He hated it. He had spent a lifetime going his own way. He had always been a man of his own will, and proud of it. But now there was this strange sensation of being guided, being pulled along by feelings and forces he neither understood nor wanted. So he had headed home, resisting the urge to look within and see what else might be done.

He entered his apartment building and caught a faint smell in the musty air. Something more than the usual scent of dirty halls and unwashed diapers and greasy cooking. Something weird.

Manny froze when his foot touched the landing. He thought he had heard a growl. Not like one of the mangy watchdogs his neighbors kept in their apartments until management caught them. More like a hungry wild beast on the prowl. And big. Very big.

Cautiously he moved along the corridor, intently searching the stairs, the hall, the other doors on his floor. Nothing. But the building was strangely quiet. Normally this time of evening there would be a dozen televisions blaring, kids yelling, adults screaming back, with a dozen stereos and boom boxes blaring in the background. But tonight was different. Not just quiet like sleeping-quiet. Quiet like empty. Quiet like the whole building was holding its breath.

When he reached his own doorway, he stopped again, this time feeling as though a steel fist had just punched him in the chest.

His door was not just broken open. It was mauled into matchwood. Manny's mind instantly felt split in two. One side of his brain started a constant shrilling shout for him to run, get out, go anywhere, but not stay here. The other, the same old independently stubborn Manny, said to himself, yeah, sure, this is why it's so quiet. Nobody, but nobody wants to admit they saw something. Whoever did this was strong enough to know nobody would talk. Wouldn't want the same thing to happen to them. Or worse.

Manny poked his head inside the door, the other voice too loud now to let him go further. His rooms had not just been searched and tossed. They had been mauled like the door. Chewed up and spit out and left in a heap of sodden carnage.

Manny looked around and started seeing things from a different perspective, the perspective of this *new* voice. They had not been searching for something. Not really. They wanted *him*. They had done this to his apartment because they had not been able to do it to him.

Then there was another new sensation, the feeling that something had been suddenly given to him. An insight so bizarre that he knew he could never have come up with it himself.

The sudden insight told him that what he saw there in front of him was not just his things. It was his *life*. He had walked this independent path of anger and conceit with a self-absorbed swagger, so sure of his own power and abilities that he had never had time for anybody. Never needed anything but himself.

And look where it had led him. To this. To danger and darkness and ruin.

And with the realization came a choice. He could ignore what he faced and move on, replace his belongings and continue as he had up to now. But next time it would be him who was mauled and trashed and left heaped like garbage. Manny did not know how he could be so sure of this, but he was sure. This was what would happen unless he took the second choice, and followed a new path to the end. Come what may. No matter how the path drew him away from what was normal and comfortable. No matter how much control and independence he had to give up. Either he chose to bend and learn and grow, or he chose to die.

The growl sounded then. Hungry. Hunting. So close it seemed to come from inside his own head. Manny turned and fled, his feet not hitting more than one step in five. He barreled through the door, searched the night, shouted at a passing taxi.

Maybe, just maybe, he could still catch the last flight to Washington.

*T*his is beautiful!"

"Now, dear," Clarice chided. "Don't let your head be turned by these trappings. Remember, the greatest beauty resides in the hearts of believers."

But before Ariel could respond, Hale was up alongside her and saying, "Almost time, Ariel. Would you come up front with me, please?"

"Yes," she said, allowing herself to be led through the packed foyer and into the soaring sanctuary. She had wanted to tell Clarice that she had not been exclaiming over the building. What had touched her so deeply was the feeling inside the church, inside the people. Beneath the smiles and the eager chatter and the handshakes and the hugs she could feel a familiar Presence. "This is wonderful."

"Sure is," Hale agreed. "Never thought I would wind up working in a church this grand.

But Leslie has a way about him. You'll see. He looks like a movie actor and talks like a diplomat. But his heart is straight for God."

The church was indeed grand, a great stone edifice built in the last century, with a ceiling of huge interlocking beams. Along both side walls rose a proud array of stained-glass windows. Yet Ariel found the place wondrous not for what it was, but rather for what it contained. Eyes turned their way, smiles greeting Hale and then showing Ariel a calm welcome.

People were gathered for worship—old and young, of different races and colors, men and women and teens and children, some in suits and others in jeans, all joined by that which none could see yet all acknowledged. She said simply, "I love it here."

Hale gave a surprised laugh. "Why, thank you. I've only been here three months, but already I feel like this church and these people are my own."

He led her up and around to the side stairs leading past the pulpit and chairs. The empty choir rows faced down upon a curved dais, where a single spotlight shone on a gleaming golden harp. "Leslie and the deacons brought me in because they wanted to reach out to the local black community. Turn this place from an affluent, mostly white bastion into a church that ministers to the needs of all the surrounding neighborhoods. I was sort of nervous at first, but these folks have gone out of their way to greet me with the Lord's gift of love."

Ariel seated herself behind the harp and looked up at him. "It shows."

"Yeah, I guess the Lord knew what He was doing when He planted me here." He beamed at her. "You need anything?"

"I'm fine," she said, and was.

"Great." He glanced at his watch. "Then if you'll excuse me, I'll go back to my place."

The crowd settled and quieted. Reverend Townsend greeted everyone and led them in an opening prayer. Throughout, Ariel remained enclosed within the bubble of comfort, a sense that she was loved and guided and cared for and home. As she quietly tuned the strings, she wondered at the difference between the outside world and here.

"We have a guest with us tonight," Reverend Townsend said. "An unexpected special visitor. Our originally planned musician was unable to join us, but a wonderful replacement has literally just stepped off the bus from Philadelphia. Ariel here is accompanying Sister Clarice, of whom many of you have heard me speak. They are here to help us get our new projects up and running." Leslie Townsend had a genuinely nice smile. "We had to hurry back from the station so fast that I did not even think to ask what Ariel wanted to play for us. Ariel?"

What indeed? She found her question lofted upward, and the response granted to her upon a wave of the same peace that filled the hall. "A song of praise."

"How wonderful." Another smile, then, "I am sure we will all want to stop by afterward and thank her for helping out at the last moment like this."

As the pastor seated himself Ariel adjusted the harp to her shoulder and ran through the strings. Then she closed her eyes. There waiting for her was that same peaceful Presence that had answered her question, a gentle guiding Spirit. Ariel fitted her fingers to the strings and let the still, small voice lead her into song.

She played of her longing for what she had left behind, the constancy of all that her home possessed. Of love beyond measure, peace without end. A light so total that no sun was required. A city of crystal and gold. A place for all. For *all*.

The song became a river, a flowing melody of praise and worship and prayerful longing, a tide of sound which in truth had neither beginning nor end. She simply joined with what always was, always will be, her strings chiming to the sound of unheard voices singing eternal praise to the King.

The Spirit within the great hall began to move, flowing with the music, filling the chapel with voices that people heard not with their ears, but rather with their hearts. Singing in time to Ariel's playing, a heavenly chorus that rose and soared on gossamer wings.

The entire chamber moved beyond the borders of time and space, of earthly woe and worry. For all who came with open honest hearts there was a moment of joining, an instant of glimpsing beyond the veil, of hearing the voice of promise and fulfillment, and knowing it was there with them, filling them with a love that was theirs for all eternity.

The message was given, the gift received. The song did not diminish, but rather soared ever higher, flying toward the unseen heavens, beyond the reach of human ears and hearts, higher and higher and higher until the final note was a chiming almost at the limit of awareness. Yet all knew that it was not the last. It was only the beginning. The first note of a song they would hear and carry with them always. Forever to be sung in praise of the One.

*M*anny was being followed. He knew it. The sensation was stronger than it had been outside the pawnshop. Manny did his weaving dance through the evening crowds filling the airport terminal, his ticket clutched in one hand like a lifeline. He dodged one of the electric carts carrying old people, jogged alongside it, glanced back and forth and to both sides, saw nothing that raised the alarm. But somebody was there. He could feel it. Somebody was after him.

Or something.

Manny sighed with genuine relief as he heard his flight's final boarding call. He raced down the concourse, feeling as though the breath of whatever had growled in his apartment was nipping at his heels. He slowed long enough for the attendant to snag his ticket, then fled down the boarding ramp and into the plane. His breath was loud in his ears as he walked down the aisle, his heart jumping more from the fright than the run.

Then he was aware once more of the invisible guiding hand. Right when he least expected it, there between the crowded rows, the flight attendant already talking over the loudspeaker. Again there was a sense of an unseen force surrounding him, reaching down and gently directing him. Crazy.

He checked his ticket for the seat number, slid into his place, breathed a sigh of relief. It was good to be leaving town for a while. His home turf was definitely getting to be a risky place to hang.

He glanced over at the man seated beside him. Big, burly, barrel-chested. Biker's T-shirt. Fists like human hammers, all gnarled and knotted. Holding a book and turning the flimsy little pages, his forehead creased in concentration. Not even acknowledging the outside world, oblivious as the plane started rolling away from the terminal. Manny leaned over, gave the book a casual glance, jerked back. The Bible. Just like he'd seen as a kid, when he had sought shelter from a heavy storm inside a street mission. Manny didn't know any other book that had those double columns and fancy red printing here and there.

He leaned back down again just to make sure, pretended to scratch his ankle while scanning the page, recognized the name Jesus. Yeah, had to be. The guy was sitting there on a plane reading the Bible. Amazing.

This time the guy noticed him. "You want to read along with me?"

Manny straightened up, did the casual stretch, no big deal. Palmed his ticket stub, read the seat number, no mistake, this was his place. "No, you go ahead."

"That's okay." The big guy slung this little ribbon across the page, closed the Book. "I can read anytime. What's your name?"

"Manny." Sitting there next to the Hulk, and the guy wants to play polite. Manny didn't argue, didn't even lie about his name.

"Mine's John. John Roskovitz." Offered his hand. "You a believer?"

Manny watched his hand be swallowed, felt strength behind the grip, but no menace. Not in the hand, not in the eyes, not in the voice. Guy with a bruiser's face, scar across his forehead and a nose broken so often it had been set at a permanent angle, but eyes that shone with a gentle light. Didn't make sense. "Not really."

"Know what you mean," the guy said agreeably. "Been there, done that. A lot."

"Yeah?" Manny glanced at his ticket stub again. Not because he thought maybe he had it wrong. No. Because he had that sense of being guided into this meeting and this contact. Crazy.

"Years and years of it," Roskovitz confirmed. "All those guys, they stand up there and tell you how it felt bad and they didn't understand why they did it. Not me. I did it because I was having a ball."

Manny felt himself being invited to relax, let down his constant guards, talk to somebody who *understood*. Normally, a stranger this size, he'd be around the corner and out of sight and gone. Not this time. "So what happened?"

"So I found something better." The guy lifted his Book. "Couldn't go both ways at the same time. Had to make a choice."

A *choice*. Manny recalled the moment in his apartment doorway, felt himself shiver.

Roskovitz noticed the change. "Something the matter?"

Manny started to deny it. But there was something about this stranger and this moment that invited him to open up. "I think maybe I got a problem."

The guy slid the Book into the pocket of the seat in front of him, crossed massive arms. "One thing I learned about problems," he said. "They're a lot easier to handle if two people carry the load."

There it was again, that sense of an invitation. Of comfort being offered, and not just from the guy. From the moment. Manny swallowed, felt the pressure of years of holding back, standing alone, being his own man. But somewhere deep inside a door was being opened, one he didn't even know existed before that moment.

He said, "I think I'm being followed."

"Yeah?" John showed only mild surprise. "You done something?"

"You kidding?" Manny had to smile. "I've done it all."

"Know what you mean, know what you mean," the guy murmured. Eyes still open and kindly. No judgment, no condemnation. Just sitting there, smiling through the roar of the takeoff, nodding a continual invitation for Manny to open up, let it out.

But still it was hard. Manny had never spoken to anybody like this before, not in his life.

"See, I found this pigeon, talk about out of it. Picked her pockets, came up with this thing, I dunno, I thought it was some kinda credit card. But when I stuck it in the bank machine, wham, I was *gone*. I mean outta here." Manny stopped, inspected the incongruous face with its hard angles of brutal power and eyes of luminous light. "That make any sense to you?"

"Might do," the guy said easily. "But you just keep on, I like the sound of your voice."

"Ever since then, I don't know, there's been one thing after another. It feels like," Manny tried to shape the air in front of him as he went on, "like I'm being sorta *guided*. Not like, okay, here, take my hand and let's go see what's down the corner. More like, this is something I maybe oughta think about, even if it don't make no sense at all."

"An opportunity," the guy said, speaking more quietly now that the plane was leveling off.

Manny had to stop and stare. The guy was not only listening. He was understanding so well it was almost like he was hearing what Manny did not know how to put into words.

Roskovitz waited with him for a time, then urged gently, "So what did you do?"

"Sometimes I took it, you know, whatever it was that I felt like was there for me," Manny replied, his voice a little weak from the surprise that somebody cared enough to search out the deeper meaning. "But it's hard. I mean, really hard. I feel like I'm fighting with myself."

Roskovitz nodded. "Hardest part of the struggle is at the turning. Up to then, you're just moving with the flow. But you start to turn, then all the forces that held you tight start getting angry. Like they don't want to let you go."

His pride pricked, Manny started to object, declare himself his own man. Then he thought about watching the shadows coalesce in the bar, about hearing that growl in his own apartment, and he kept still. All the forces that held him tight. Manny felt a chill burn like dry ice in his gut.

"Long as you're going the way *they* want you to," Roskovitz went on, "everything's fine. They let you think you're on your own. Strong and powerful enough to face whatever comes. King of all you survey, like that."

Manny gave a tiny nod, a single jerk, almost against his will. This guy was reading him like a book, showing him things he sort of felt, but never thought about before. It left him uncomfortable. And scared. But wanting to hear more just the same.

"Then something happens, and all of a sudden there's this fork in the road. And you think maybe you ought to take the other way, but soon as you do, all these forces are up in arms. You're no longer part of them, see. You're joining the opposition."

"I'm not joining nothing," Manny denied.

The guy just looked at him, the gentle gaze now piercing. "You can't stand in the middle of the road," he said. "You gotta keep moving, gotta make that choice. And once you choose, you've got to *commit*. You don't, they'll keep after you, those forces. When you're weak or not looking, they'll drag you back. And once they do, you're lost."

The truth of the guy's words resounded through Manny like the tolling of a great bell. Like the time had come, and the bell of his life was sounding. *Bong, bong, bong*, like that, pealing in great thunderous power that caused his whole being to shake until he could scarcely get out the words. "So what do I do?"

Roskovitz leaned forward and plucked the

Bible from the seat pocket in front of him. "Let me tell you what it says in here."

*T*he night had a physical presence, soft and vibrant and full of mystery. Ariel lay in her bed, separated from Clarice by a nightstand and her churning thoughts. So much to take in. So much to learn.

She recalled scenes she had witnessed and sighed quietly, "I just don't understand."

Clarice shifted in her bed, said sleepily, "Understand what, dear?"

They were in the upstairs guest room of Reverend Townsend's home, a nice red-brick house on a quiet side street not far from the church. Outside their window a car passed along the silent street, a dog barked, a nightbird sounded its lonely cry. Inside all was warmth and comfort.

"Everywhere I look," Ariel said quietly, "I see God's blessed creation overlaid with, well . . ."

"Darkness," Clarice said for her. "Darkness and unseen shadows."

Ariel looked over, searching the night. "How can you *stand* it here?"

"You are truly the strangest girl I have ever come across in all my days. The Spirit moves in you. After what I've seen at the bus station and hearing you play the harp, there's no doubt in my mind about that. But, Lord, your questions." Clarice chuckled softly. "Where were you raised, on a lofty mountaintop up above the clouds?"

Ariel struggled with how to reply, settled on, "Yes."

"Well, it wouldn't surprise me one bit." The bed creaked as Clarice raised herself up to a sitting position. "Now listen here. We live in a fallen world. Our job is not to worry over that, because doing so won't get us anywhere. Our job is to be servants of the Holy One and make little openings for His grace to come through and touch the world around us. And our strongest tool is prayer. We must pray and pray and pray without ceasing, filling ourselves and our surroundings with His gracious love."

Ariel listened and heard more than just the woman's words. She heard the strength, the simple conviction, the years of struggle and giving and living for more than just herself. "You are a very special woman, Clarice."

"I'm tired is what I am. A woman my age needs her rest. Now you close your eyes and we'll have us a time of prayer. Then I want you to turn your worries over to the One who can handle them and get some sleep."

So what brings you down here, anyway?"

"Hard to say," Manny replied weakly, and

pushed his breakfast plate to one side. They were seated in the restaurant of a cheap motel not far from the Washington bus station. The night before, Manny had said he needed to go straight there, he needed to find somebody. John Roskovitz had shrugged those massive shoulders and said that was fine with him, he'd be working down in that area the next day, anyway. Taking it easy, not pushing, just along for the ride.

But the bus station had been a nonstarter. Manny had searched the place from top to bottom, talked to some homeboys hanging out, found no sign of the girl and no one who had seen her.

Unable to think of anything else he could do, Manny had agreed to John's suggestion and walked with the big man to the motel. He had gone to bed tired and frustrated and angry, feeling both used and confused.

And had woken up feeling exactly the same way.

Manny shook his head when the waitress came by offering hot coffee, then asked Roskovitz, "So what about you?"

"There's a church not far from here," Roskovitz replied. "They're setting up a relief center for local kids. Rich crowd, big church, you know how it is, don't have any idea what they're up against. They see these kids hanging around every day and never talked to one of them in their lives. But the Spirit works where it will, and from what I hear these folks have been hit hard. So they heard about some work I've done in Philadelphia, bringing kids off the street and getting them started with life. Asked me to come down and help them get set up."

"Great," Manny said dully. The Spirit. Guy just tosses it out like he's on a personal first-name basis with something or someone he's never even seen. This was another thing that had really messed with his head the night before, all the stuff Roskovitz had laid on him, pointing to place after place in the Bible, laying it all out, saying this was what he had to do. *Had* to do. Not like, okay, this is something maybe he should think about. No, it was, okay, you want to get a life, you've got to do this and this and this.

Crazy.

Manny felt the old urges building. Pushing him up and away and out of there. Back to the street. Back to where he was his own man, not having some former biker trying to scare him with stuff out of a book two thousand years dead. No, this whole scene wasn't for him.

He slid from the booth, avoided John's eyes until he was on his feet. "Look, I gotta go check some things out."

"Sure you do."

The quiet words swung Manny's gaze up. Finding the big guy just sitting there calmly, watching him with that same level gaze, like there wasn't a single solitary thing about Manny he didn't know. "Yeah, well, look, it's been great and all that."

Roskovitz nodded once, twice, three times. "Hard to take it all in, ain't it."

"No, hey, I really appreciate it and all, but you know, I got a lot of stuff to take care of."

"Big world out there," John agreed. He pulled a pen and paper from his pocket, scribbled, handed it over. "That's the name of the church where I'll be. You don't find me, ask for the assistant pastor. Guy by the name of Hale."

"Hale. Right. Sure." Stuffing the paper in his pocket. At least until he was out the door and around the corner. "Hey, good luck with the kids."

"Hard as it is, you need to remember that the turning in the road won't be there for long," Roskovitz said. "Chances like this come and go and leave you trapped worse than before. You need to grab it while you can."

"Yeah, hey, this is really fascinating," Manny said, feeling the itch build until his feet were ready to fly, with or without the rest of him. "But listen, I gotta take off."

"Make the turning while you still can," John Roskovitz said, the words flying after Manny in his race for the door. "I'll be praying that you do."

*M*anny did not walk the streets. He paraded. His steps were a fiery dance of independence. Free from the worries and the pushing and the crazy talk, his own man again. Free.

Washington, D.C. He already loved this

place. The avenue he walked seemed to split the town like a knife. On one side was wealth, and all the possibilities such riches brought a guy like him. On the other side was ghetto city, drugs and gangs and homeboy turf. The perfect place to hide when he had netted the wares and needed a place to chill.

He pushed through a cluster of pigeons, looked at them standing there; they seemed afraid that one small turn would bring them face-to-face with their worst nightmare. He grinned to himself. Yeah, he was all right again, his head back on straight. All that time, what he had really needed most was a change of scene.

Manny did not watch where he was going, did not need to, not now, not while he was cruising, taking the air, getting the feel of his new home. Every once in a while a little drift of what he had been hearing and thinking about those past few days would pop into his mind. He would push it away even before the thought and the feeling could form and congeal, shoulder it out, and just walk a little faster. Shoving out all that crazy stuff and the strange way it shook him.

He danced along the crowded sidewalk,

decided without thinking that he could take the next turning, get on a side street where the going was easier. Taking the corner by half-climbing a street sign, swinging up and around and away, drawing gasps from the passersby, out of sight before the people fully realized what they had just seen.

The side street led away from the glitz and toward the ghetto, the change sudden. He had a feeling a lot of the city was like that, battle lines drawn almost everywhere. His dance was a strut now, showing the locals he was a man in the know, somebody they didn't want to mess with. Taking another turn, feeling the tension and the anger and the hardship and the drugged-out stress, drawing it in like he did his air, feeding on it. This was his world, the place he could call his own. The same in every city, a dark jungle even at noon, a tangled, fear-ridden strip where only the strong survived. Another turn, not really seeing, just moving with the flow and reveling in the power that seethed with this sense of rebellious freedom.

Suddenly he halted, the world drawing back into focus. He found himself standing in front of a storefront doorway. Manny looked around, had the sense of abruptly coming awake. Bizarre, like he had been heading here all the time, which was impossible because he hadn't even been looking where he was going. Angry now, pushing at the thoughts and the door at the same time, not paying attention to the words written on smoked glass in pointy, flowing gold letters: *The Sorcerer's Apprentice.*

A voice from an alcove to his right suddenly said, "Ah, Manny, excellent, excellent."

Manny spun about. "Eh, whatsthatyousaid?"

"We've been looking everywhere for you." A delicately slender man pushed through the curtain and walked toward him.

Manny took a step back. Then he realized he was moving *away* from the door, his carefully honed survival instincts failing him in the clutch. "How'd you know my name?"

"Oh, you have quickly become quite famous in our circles." He was elegantly turned out, his dark hair caught in a silver ring and well-trimmed beard flecked with gray. He wore a flowing red silk shirt over black trousers tucked into fold-down boots. "How on earth have you been?"

"Swell." Manny gave the room a quick

scan. Dusty old tomes rose to the ceiling, stacked in careless abandon, some of them bound in metal and embossed with strange symbols. The same symbols decorated the ceiling and hung from the walls in ornately scrolled frames. Maps that made no sense were framed alongside the symbols, with great dragons spouting fire and faces blowing stormclouds and edges inscribed in strange script. Brass instruments were arranged under the counter glass and stacked behind the register, all of it beyond weird.

The fellow reached out a ring-encrusted hand. "We've been so terribly worried."

"Yeah?" Manny watched the hand like he would a snake, making no move toward it. His skin crawled like it had that day in the pawnshop. "Who's we?"

"Why, everyone." The man masked the retreat of his hand by smoothing down his slicked-back hair. "We had absolutely no idea where you had gotten to. It was like you had dropped off the edge of our little world."

Our world. The word grated on his nerves like steel fingernails dragged down a mile-long blackboard. *Our* world. "Somebody's been following me. I knew it all the time."

"Oh, if only we could have." The eyes glit-tered and stretched with the thin smile. "But you moved away from us, you naughty boy. You vanished. Now how on earth did you do that, especially when you had something we needed so badly? You can imagine how *worried* everybody has been."

"Yeah?" Manny felt the eyes drilling him to the spot. There was neither time nor space to pre-tend he didn't know what the man was after. He had no choice but to go back to his old palaver. No choice at all. "So I'm here," he bluffed. "You gonna pay, or is this just all hot air?"

"Oh, my dear young friend, we will pay *anything*. Name your price. Riches, fame, for-tune, it's yours. All of it."

All of it. Everything he had ever wanted. Somehow he knew the fellow was telling the truth. But the promise brought him nothing but a chilling doubt. "So what's so great about this thing?"

The fellow misread his hesitation, and took a step toward Manny, his voice a sibilant hiss. "You do have it, don't you?"

Manny shrugged, worked to keep the qua-ver from his voice. "Yeah, sure. I might. Somewhere safe."

"Of course. My, or perhaps I should say *our* superiors will be so relieved." The tension rose a notch. "What the card is, hmmm, I think you know. A young man of your many talents would certainly have tried it by now." Another step, the glittering eyes so close that the dark center points opened to become bottomless wells. "You cannot imagine how long they have sought this key. It is the *bridge*, my young friend. *The* bridge. Now the banner of war can be raised against all we despise."

"Hey, that's great." Struggling to get out the words. Feeling a band tightening across his chest. Wanting to turn and flee. Knowing he had to. But unable to move. "I kinda figured it was something like that."

"Of course you did." The pools of his eyes opened further, reaching out to encompass the entire chamber, drawing him in, pulling him down farther and farther, sucking the life and the will and the ability to think right from Manny's body. "Now tell me, won't you, where is the card?"

Manny teetered on the brink, ready to fall into the pit, more terrified and trapped than he had ever been in his life. He heard it again then, the hungry growl, and knew without any doubt whatsoever that the beast was there, and hungry, and waiting to devour him whole.

Suddenly Manny glimpsed something. An image came and went so swiftly he scarcely realized it had been there. The image was of John Roskovitz's gentle gray eyes. And in that same instant there was the sense of half hearing softly spoken words. A prayer. A prayer spoken for *him*.

The fellow jerked back as though electrocuted. One hand clutched his chest, the other reached for the countertop for support, and he shrilled, "What was *that?*"

With the power of a lightning bolt, Manny was freed. He gasped a single breath as the room sprang into focus. Then he leapt for the door, clawed for the handle even as he heard the fellow scream, "Wait!" But Manny was waiting for nobody. Not now. He flung open the door and was gone.

Only when he had fled down block after block and stopped in a doorway to scan all directions did it hit him *hard*. A realization so strong that it could not be denied. A *knowing*. The whole time he had been running away from one thing, he had been running toward another. One or the other, just like Roskovitz had told him. He had to choose.

A second bolt of *knowing* blasted him, a voice so strong and commanding it was heard even though it was silent, the impossible made real. It spoke just one word, but a word that shattered his entire world.

Choose.

"Arise, my soul, arise," were the first words Ariel heard the next morning. She turned over and saw Clarice standing by the window, her arms lifted to the rising sun. Her eyes were closed, her voice calm and quiet and full of joy. "My God, my God, for this day do I give you thanks."

"Amen," Ariel said quietly as she sat up in bed, swinging her feet to the floor. She bowed her head, and in a quiet sweeping gift of peace, she felt the sun rise within her own heart.

"With confidence I now draw nigh," Clarice said. "With heartfelt thanksgiving I shake off my guilty fears. Before the throne I stand and give thanks for the eternal offering."

"Amen," Ariel intoned, and in the growing strength of day felt the silent bonds of worship join the two of them together. This was more than a prayer for her. This was a *lesson*. She both heard the prayer and felt the sense of growing harmony. All was being brought together through this act of private communion. The confusion that had marred her every

114

experience since arriving dispersed, and once again all was being brought together through eternal love, eternal light, eternal healing. She intoned once again, "Amen."

"Your pardoning voice I hear, O Father. Your grace reaches out to embrace me, the fallen child. Your welcoming herald calls me home."

"Amen," Ariel whispered, and knew a longing so fierce that her memory suddenly flashed alert.

When Clarice finished her prayers, she smiled a warm greeting and said, "I can't recall the last time I have slept so long. The trip must have tired me out more than I thought."

Ariel nodded and announced, "St. Mark's Hospice for the Dying. That's where Miss Simpkins is working. I've remembered."

*T*he old gypsy dreamer rose from his trash pile and straightened his battered fedora. Manny glanced up from the crumpled paper he had pulled from his pocket, but was too caught up in his thoughts and his hurry to notice as the crooked-featured man fell into step beside him.

Bad to the bone. That was the way he had always thought of himself. A song by that name had been a theme he had chanted through long nights of carousing. Bad to the bone. The utter *wrongness* of it all now left him feeling so twisted he had to fight not to stumble.

Manny retraced his steps the best he could, his growing inward vision spurring him to hurry despite the weakness in his limbs. All that time, all those years, chasing after a good time, fueled by anger and bitter cynicism, certain he was strong enough to be his own man, unfettered by all that held the rest of the world down.

What a joke. What a *lie*.

His anger had been a trap. His so-called independence had left him nothing but blind. His good times had been the grease lubricating the slide to doom.

Then something caught his eye.

He stopped and realized that he was gasping for air. His legs felt encased in lead. He swung about, saw the gypsy drunk leering in his direction, one arm reaching out, begging for a dime. Then Manny felt the hair on the nape of his neck prickle upward as he caught sight of the man's shadow. It crawled along the earth behind the drunk, but instead of holding to the outstretched form it weaved and beckoned, drawing other shadows to come and join and grow and strengthen. The shadow linked with others hauled from alleys and cellars and doorways until its arms began to lengthen and grow and stretch across the street and along the sidewalk and over the building like two great crablike claws reaching out and around where Manny stood.

Manny turned and tried to run, but his footsteps were faltering and slow. He felt as though the very earth were trying to draw him deep inside. He craned and searched but could not find a sign he recognized, nor any indication of where he might be. His panic-stricken mind held to that thought as he fought and struggled onward, his legs carrying him in stumbling half-steps toward the corner. He *had* to get to that church where Roskovitz said he was working.

From the corner of his eye he spotted the shadows racing forward, dark tentacles that split and grew and lengthened, a beast from the deep ready to ensnare and draw him down.

Manny lifted his face to the sky, his neck so taut that the tendons stood out like cables, and screamed, *"Help me!"*

The tentacles faltered, the load on his legs lightened, and he made the corner. Manny gripped the building's edge, pulled himself around, and spotted a steeple up ahead. He gave a cry of pure relief and ran forward.

M iss Simpkins," the hospice director said, beaming at the name. "Oh what a lovely lady she was."

Was. Clarice turned in time to see the word register on Ariel's features. The young woman swallowed, then asked meekly, "She's gone?"

"Just yesterday. And what a pity, too. She said she was called back home, I forget exactly why, but it had to be something urgent. Right in the middle of the afternoon shift, she came and told me she had to leave that very minute."

The director was a woman in her fifties, plump and orderly and strong. The hospice itself occupied what once had been a grand private residence. Now there was the sense of settled quiet about the entrance hall, as well as the same strength that radiated from the director. She wore the weight of her work with the calm certainty of one not bearing the burden alone. "We shall miss her."

"Yes," Ariel said simply, her face slack with disappointment. Then she picked herself up and asked, "Would it be all right if I visited the area where she worked?"

The director looked doubtful. "I'm not sure that's a good idea. We are a home for those who have nowhere else to go, you see. Some of them are not happy about their fate."

"I understand," Ariel said quietly. "But it would be nice to see what she was doing before . . ." she hesitated, then finished, "before she left."

"Ariel worked in a hospital," Clarice offered, seeing how much this fragile contact

with her absent friend meant to her.

"Oh, well, in that case." The matron pointed through the pair of doors to her right. "She worked with patients in the central ward, just along there."

"Thank you," Ariel said, her voice quietly submissive. With eyes downcast, she slipped through the doors and was gone.

"What a strange young lady," the director murmured, her gaze questioning.

Clarice nodded her agreement, then explained how she had met Ariel. The director listened with the patience of one used to the chore of waiting. Clarice finished with, "I have so many questions about her myself. But one thing I can say for certain. She is a child of God."

The director opened her mouth to respond, but before she said anything the doors popped open once more, admitting a young nurse with the eyes of an ancient. "Did you send someone back here?"

Both women turned together. The director demanded, "Is something the matter?"

"It's the strangest thing," the nurse replied, shaking her head. "But until I saw her, I thought for sure Miss Simpkins was back."

Clarice followed the director and the nurse through the doors, down the hall, and into a cheerfully decorated room. It had the high ceiling and great windows of what once had been a formal parlor. Now a series of movable screens offered the choice of privacy to the seven beds, all of them occupied. But the screens were pulled back now, permitting in the brilliant summer sun.

Clarice arrived in the doorway just as Ariel was rising from having knelt beside a bed. Clarice knew a moment of alarm when she realized the old woman lying there was crying.

But as Ariel rose, the old woman refused to let go of her hands. Ariel gave a smile so gentle it twisted Clarice's heart. Ariel bent over the wizened figure and spoke a few words and the old woman nodded back, her peaked chin quivering. Ariel slid one hand free, rested it on the old woman's forehead, and closed her eyes. The old woman released a gasping sob. Ariel opened her eyes, bent down, and kissed the parchment-covered cheek. The old woman smiled through her tears as Ariel turned to the next bed, where a young child lay with arms already outstretched to greet her.

Clarice watched and felt herself drawn

into the scene, melding with both prayer and penitent as Ariel knelt beside the second bed. She had the impression that all light in the room was focused upon the kneeling figure. The child had eyes made overlarge by suffering, hollowed and aching in their unspoken need. She watched Ariel's face with unblinking intensity. And as she did, the child's dark stains of pain and fatigue eased, the pinched features softened, the shadows drew away.

Ariel raised her head and opened her eyes. She spoke words so soft that only the tone carried to where the trio stood. The child managed a little smile and a smaller nod. Ariel reached out and stroked the little forehead. The child caught the hand and held it to her cheek. Clutching at more than just flesh, the eyes searched for what remained unseen to all but her questing gaze. Ariel spoke again, then reached over with both hands, her arms encircling the little form and drawing it to her breast. The child closed her eyes and released herself to the comfort of knowing love.

A small sound drew Clarice's attention away from the scene. She glanced up to see the nurse standing beside her, hands to her mouth, eyes overflowing. Clarice turned her attention back, full of the moment's grace.

She watched as Ariel went from bed to bed, carrying the light and the love with her. Received by each in silent communion, the message given so softly that it was meant for only one pair of ears, each time unique, each time the same. Sharing all she had with those in need. A prayer so strong and luminous that fear was vanquished, pain dimmed, and hope rekindled.

Then, as Clarice watched Ariel rise from the final bed, the Spirit whispered to her heart. Clarice looked at the young woman, and she saw.

anny!" The scarred giant crossed the church foyer with a grin and out-

stretched hand. "You're a sight for sore eyes. Welcome, brother!"

Manny gripped John Roskovitz's hand like a lifeline. He gasped, "They're after me."

"Of course they are." The grin carried the wisdom of shared experience. "You think they're just gonna give up and let you be? After all this time you been one of the lost tribe?" Roskovitz shook his head. "They want you back, Manny. Ain't nothing in their agreement says you can quit when you want."

Manny's free hand reached for a hold on the biker T-shirt. "What'm I gonna do?"

"Calm down for a start," Roskovitz said, gently prying himself loose. "They can't follow you in here."

A ray of hope pierced his fear. "They can't?"

"This is God's holy temple, filled with the power of prayer and living faith," John assured him. "Come on, there's somebody I want you to meet."

He led Manny down a side hall and into an office where a strong young black man sat talking on the phone. When he set the receiver down, John said, "Hale, like you to meet a new seeker. Manny, this is the guy that asked me down to Washington."

"Nice to meet you, Manny," Hale said, coming around the desk with an outstretched hand.

"Yeah, likewise," he mumbled. So many smiles. So much difference from what he had seen outside. Manny's inbred caution urged him to withdraw, but he was lured outward by the gentle luminosity in those dark eyes, the same light he saw in John's gaze.

"The brother's coming from a place I've been myself," John said. "Needs a little help from the God squad."

Hale nodded as though the words made perfect sense. "What did you have in mind?"

John's hand rested strong and reassuring on Manny's shoulder. "I think maybe we ought to gather the strongest prayer warriors we can lay our hands on, help this brother set his burdens down."

I went into the ward, and I thought for a moment I was going to drown in all that pain and fear," Ariel told Clarice. "And then I remembered what you have been teaching me about prayer. So I prayed. And you were right."

They were driving back to the church in the car Reverend Townsend had lent them. Clarice listened to what Ariel was saying and waited. She knew she was going to have to speak, to say the words, but she did not know how.

"Now I think I understand why I was called here. The lesson of prayer is at the heart of faith. I never understood that before. But I do now. It is not just a responsibility. Prayer is a gift. Prayer is our way of drawing heaven into our home and our lives here on earth." Ariel looked out her side window and said, "The Father truly does dwell among us here."

"God is everywhere," Clarice replied. So

much was coming clear now.

"I forgot that," Ariel admitted. "No, not forgot, I simply did not comprehend. When I arrived, I found so much that was not of Him, I thought He had no place here. That He had made the world and then left it. But I was wrong. He is *always* here. And everywhere. Just waiting for hearts to open to Him and let Him enter."

"And then work through that heart on other hungry souls," Clarice added.

"I understand that now, thanks to you." Ariel turned from the window. "I carry the Lord with me everywhere I go. It is the one gift I shall always have, the one I can never give enough of to others." She was silent a long moment, then added, "If it is His will for me to stay and work here, then I accept it. Because now I understand."

Clarice found herself unable to wait any longer. She pulled over to the side of the street and parked. It took a long moment to release her grip on the wheel and turn to Ariel, and when she did she found the young woman watching her, quietly expectant.

Clarice took a long breath, then said solemnly, "I think I know who you are, Ariel."

She gestured with one unsteady hand at the world outside the car. "You are not from here at all."

"No," Ariel agreed, matching her solemn gaze. And she explained the story of her arrival, of her mission, of all that had happened since.

There was a long silence before Clarice remembered to breathe. After that she was able to ask, "What is heaven like?"

"It is home," Ariel replied simply. "Our only home."

"*Our* home," Clarice whispered, and seemed to give a little shiver. Another silence, then, "Do you know Jesus?"

Ariel's face bloomed with a light that suffused everything around her. "Yes," she replied. "I know the Lamb. And He knows me."

Awe gave Clarice's aged features the brightness of a little child's. "What is He like?"

Ariel returned the open gaze with a smile and the words, "You will see."

hat do I do?"

"Just answer the call, brother." John had not let go of Manny for an instant since his arrival. "The message is already there in your heart. Can you feel it?"

"I guess so. Yeah." Manny's teeth were chattering so hard he could scarcely get out the words.

They were seated in a side chamber, together with a circle of perhaps two dozen men and women, joined in hand and in Spirit. All eyes rested on Manny. Not in accusation, not in judgment. In *joining*.

"We're right here with you," John said. "Walking the walk, helping you take that first step. The turning is just there in front of you. Are you ready?"

Manny managed a nod. The trembling had spread throughout his entire frame, a shivering that moved in waves from the inside out.

Pushing away all the dregs of who he was and what he had done. Making room for what was now to come.

"Just let the love rain down from above," John murmured. "Let the light shine for you, straightening out the path, showing you who you are."

Who he was. Empty of all that he had called himself, he felt a new wind begin blowing through him. Strange and frightening in its awesome power, yet blissfully welcome.

"I will start with a little prayer," John said. "Then let your heart speak for you. Admit you've done wrong, that you see it now and you're ready to turn away from the sin and the tainted ways."

A pair of voices began praying softly across the way. Manny could not hear the words. But he could *feel* them. Their prayers joined with this newfound power, a silent shout of joy blowing through his heart.

"Ask the Lord God to enter your life," John went on. "Accept the gift of salvation offered by His Son."

More and more quiet voices joined in prayer, heads bowing around the room as one after another the brothers and sisters allowed the Spirit to speak through them. The silent chorus grew ever stronger in Manny's heart, a witness to the power of what was now arriving.

"Ask for His protection," John said. "Ask for His cleansing and His love and His guidance. Ask for whatever you want, Manny. It is your right."

His *right*. Manny did not consciously drop his head. The gentle guiding hand was there, and this time he did not resist. He heard himself begin to speak, but he could not hear. His entire being was vibrating to the power of what grew within his awakening heart.

Freedom.

*I*t's so quiet," Clarice whispered, the silent church causing her to lower her voice.

"Where is everybody?"

"I don't know," Ariel replied quietly. "But something's going on. I can feel it."

"Sure is," announced a hearty voice. They turned as a bent old man shuffled out, pushing a mop in front of him. "They're in a room back along that corridor there, and they're praying their hearts out."

Ariel nodded, as though she already knew the answer. "Why aren't you in there with them?"

"Don't need to be." The janitor shambled over to his wheeled bucket, sloshed the mop in the water, pulled it up and twisted it dry in one practiced motion. "I can pray just as strong out here. 'Sides, I got work to do."

Clarice felt the coming of unspoken wisdom, a gift of insight beyond herself. She glanced at Ariel and let herself be guided into saying, "My name is Clarice, and this is my friend Ariel. She needs praying over."

Both the janitor and Ariel looked up at her. But it was the old man who spoke. "That a fact?"

"Yes," Clarice replied. "She has fallen from heaven and wants to return to God's sweet embrace."

The old man looked at Ariel. "That

true, what she's saying?"

"Yes," Ariel said, her eyes big as saucers. "Yes, it is."

"Well, ain't a soul on earth who hasn't stumbled and fallen at one time or another. Happens to the strongest believer." The janitor set his mop back in the bucket, turned his full attention on Ariel. "What's important now is that the erring child wants to be reconciled. Returned to the fold and joined again with the Maker of all."

"Oh yes," Ariel said. Stronger now. "I want that more than anything."

"I hear the truth in your voice," the janitor said, and wiped his hands on his trouser legs. "Wait here just one minute, let me see if they're ready to help another."

When the janitor had shuffled off, Ariel walked over and grasped Clarice's hand. "Do you really think it will work?"

"Ask and you shall receive," Clarice repeated. "My whole life has been built upon the truth in those words."

*T*he janitor came back with one of the biggest men Clarice had ever seen. "Which one of you sisters is Ariel?"

"I am." Her voice was soft, yet strong as the wind.

"I'm John Roskovitz. He shook hands with her, then with Clarice. His eyes were bright as midnight lanterns. "Got to tell you, the Spirit's strong in there. Strong."

"That's just exactly what we need," Clarice replied for them both.

"Never can tell who God is gonna use," John said, ushering them down the hall. "Might even be you or me, we let Him have His way."

They entered the room to find a group of smiling people clustered around one young man, whose face was suffused with newfound wonder. Clarice felt Ariel start at the sight of him. The young man glanced over, jerked just as Ariel had, and exclaimed, "I don't believe this."

135

"Better stop with that right smart," the janitor said, shuffling in and seating himself. "Belief is something you can't have enough of."

"It *is* you," Ariel said.

"Bet your life," the young man said. He reached into a hidden pocket of his vest, came out with a shining silver card. "This yours?"

"Oh yes." Staring at it, at him, then to Clarice, wonder filling her features. "But how—"

"Don't ask. You do *not* want to know." He walked over and placed the card in her numb fingers. "I know this is gonna sound crazy, but I gotta thank you. If it wasn't for you, I don't know where I'd be right now, but it sure wouldn't be here."

Ariel gazed at the card in her hand, said quietly, "Thank God."

The guy grinned. "I just did."

"Enough of this chatter," the janitor said from his seat. "We're keeping the Spirit waiting."

"Right." John Roskovitz turned to the group. "We've had a special request for prayers from Ariel here. Seeing as how we're all charged up, I thought maybe we should just go ahead now." He turned to her and asked, "You ready?"

"I . . ." Ariel stopped, slid the card into her pocket, said, "Yes."

"Great." The big man clapped his hands. "Okay, places everybody. Join hands, brothers and sisters, and let the Spirit move as it will."

"We thank you for the victory, Father," John intoned. Words seldom came easy to him, except in those prayers when he felt the Spirit's guidance. And never before had it been as strong as now. Never. "When we are weak, you are there for us, strong for us, there to see us through."

The murmuring around the circle was an unbroken refrain. He felt the Spirit rise within him, growing in power and focus until it lifted from his heart to his throat and into his mouth. And his words became not just his own, but more.

"Saints and angels gather nigh," he prayed, and the vista behind his closed eyelids became brilliant with a light from beyond. "Love of God, rich and pure, fill us now. Bring us home, Lord. Bring us home."

The words were spoken by a human voice, yet joined by a chorus of song and light and power. His eyes still closed, he felt as though the chamber had suddenly grown so crowded with unseen hosts that there was scarcely room left to draw breath.

Yet breathe he did, and with the air drew in a power so overwhelming that he felt lifted beyond the room. Beyond the world. "Saints and angels gather nigh," he intoned once more, the words carrying a shimmering brilliance he both felt and saw with his outpouring heart. "Love of God, rich and pure, fill us now. Bring us home, Lord. Bring us home."

He opened his eyes to find all others raising their heads, drawn back by the chiming of a distant silver bell.

Ariel had clearly heard it too. For when she rose to her feet, her eyes shone with the same illumination that filled the room. "I have to go," she said, her voice singing with unmistakable joy. "It is time."

She looked from one face to the other. "Thank you," she said. "Thank you all."

The room watched her cross to where Manny sat, reached in her pocket, and came out with the slender card. "I want you to have this."

He drew back in genuine fear. "Not me. Not ever."

"Go ahead," she urged. "It's been changed. It's yours now. No one will ever try to take it from you."

Hesitantly Manny reached out, took it, looked with widening eyes as he held it up. The card was now perfectly clear, save for silver letters scrolled across the surface. Manny read quietly, "Jude 20 and 21. 'Dear friends, build yourselves up in your most holy faith, and pray in the Holy Spirit. Keep yourselves in God's love as you wait for the mercy of our Lord Jesus Christ to bring you to eternal life.' "

As Ariel walked toward the door, Clarice asked, "But what about you?"

"Oh, I don't need the card anymore. I've learned the lesson now. The way to heaven is paved with prayer." She looked down at Clarice, her smile as soft and pure as faith. "Thanks to you, my newfound teacher and friend."

Clarice raised one hand, half in farewell,

half in entreaty for her to stay. "I will miss you, Ariel."

Ariel grasped the hand with both of hers and replied, "Not for long."